Crown Duel

Crown Duel

SHERWOOD SMITH

Book I of the Crown & Court Duet

JANE YOLEN BOOKS
HARCOURT BRACE & COMPANY
San Diego   New York   London

Requests for permission to make copies of any part of the work should be
mailed to: Permissions Department, Harcourt Brace & Company,
6277 Sea Harbor Drive, Orlando, Florida 32887-6777.

Library of Congress Cataloging-in-Publication Data
Smith, Sherwood.
Crown duel / Sherwood Smith.
p. cm.
"Jane Yolen Books."
Summary: To fulfill their father's dying wish, teenage Countess Meliara
and her brother, Branaric, organize a revolution against a greedy king.
ISBN 0-15-201608-2
[1. Fantasy.] I. Title.
PZ7.S65933Cr 1997
[Fic]—dc20 96-44193

Text set in Janson Text
Designed by Ivan Holmes

F E D C

Printed in the United States of America

This story is dedicated to my agent,
Valerie Smith.

With special thanks to my writing group,
the Foam Riders, and to Kathleen
Dalton-Woodbury, for reading this in draft

PROLOGUE

I HOPE ANY OF MY DESCENDANTS READING THIS KNOW exactly what the Covenant and the Code of War are, but there is always the chance that my story has been copied by the scribes and taken to another land that will consider Remalna distant and its customs strange.

The Covenant has to do with wood—and with Fire Sticks.

We share the land with the Hill Folk. They were here before our people came. One legend has it they were once trees, given human form by some powerful sorcerer. They certainly look more like trees than they do like people. Other stories insist they came through one of the fabled World Gates and settled here because of our trees.

For the trees in our country are unique. We have the common kinds, of course. But high in our mountains we also have the remarkable colortrees: huge, long-lived goldwoods and bluewoods and greenwoods and redwoods, so named because the grains of these trees run rich with gleaming colors.

For centuries Remalna made itself wealthy by cutting them down and selling them to other lands. But our greed nearly caused disaster. The Hill Folk, who were being driven from their homes among the trees, readied themselves to fight. Not in war, because they don't use weapons. Remalna faced a magical fight that we had no hope of winning. Peace was made only when our people promised that trees would never again be cut down. Wood would be gathered only if it fell. In return, each autumn the Hill Folk would give us Fire Sticks, which would burn by magic until well into the next summer.

Rich or poor, every family within the borders of Remalna—from the King to the poorest street sweeper—gets Fire Sticks. In proportion not to their riches but to their number. And anyone who tries to take Fire Sticks, or to sell them, somehow receives fewer the next year.

The Fire Sticks are given out by magicians from a distant council, who then disappear. There is a simple spell we say to start the fire, and to stop it—*Words of Power*, we call it, though the spell can't actually do anything else.

Since the days the Covenant was made, no more colortrees have been chopped down. What wood we use is gathered from windfall, and it is used carefully. Our old wooden furniture is treasured.

And so we've existed peacefully beside the Hill Folk for many hundred years.

Unfortunately, neighboring countries have not let us exist in peace.

For centuries we fought battles hand-to-hand. Several generations ago someone brought to our continent bows and arrows, which can kill from a distance. These changed the character of battle so much that a Code of War was agreed on by most of the countries on our continent. The only weapons permitted would be those held or thrown by hand.

When my story began, these rules had kept us relatively prosperous and in relative peace. I say "relative" because real peace and real prosperity are not possible when you are ruled by a bad king who thinks he is above all the laws.

ONE

THE BROKEN SHUTTER IN THE WINDOW CREAKED A warning. I flung myself across the table, covering as best I could my neat piles of papers, as a draft of cold wind scoured into the room. Dead leaves whispered on the stone floor, and the corners of my moat of papers rustled. Something crashed to the floor behind me. I turned my head. It was the soup bowl I'd set that morning on an old, warped three-legged stool and promptly forgotten.

The rotted blue hanging in the doorway billowed, then rippled into quiescence. The whispers and rattles in the room stilled, and I sat up with care and looked at the bowl. Could it be mended? I knew Julen would be angry with me. Julen was the blacksmith's sister, and the mother of my friend Oria. After my mother died she looked after me, and she had of late taken over cooking for us. Crockery was hard to come by these days.

I reached for the pieces, my blanket ripped—and cold leaked up my arm.

I sat back on my cushion, staring down in dismay at the huge tear at my elbow. I did not look forward to the darning task ahead—but I knew that Julen would give me one of those looks she was so good at and calmly say that practicing my darning would teach me patience.

"Mel?"

The voice was Bran's. He tapped outside the door, then lifted the hanging. "Meliara, it's time to go see Papa."

Ordinarily Branaric never called me Meliara, but I was too distracted to notice right then.

"Bran!" I leaped to my feet. "I did it—just finished! Look!" I pulled him into the room, which had once been a kind of parlor for the servants, back when the castle had had plenty of servants. Pointing proudly at the table, I said, "I know how to cheer Papa, Bran. I've found us a way to pay this year's taxes! It's taken me two days, but I really believe I have it. It'll buy us another year—you know we need another year. Look," I babbled, stooping down to tap each pile of papers. "Every village, every town in Tlanth, and what it has, what it owes, and what it needs. Not counting the gold we set aside for our Denlieff mercenaries—"

"Mel."

I looked up, my mouth still moving; but when I saw the stricken look in Bran's dark blue eyes, all the plans fled from my mind as if that cold wind had swept them into the shadowy corners with the dead leaves.

Branaric looked back at me, his face suddenly unfamiliar. My brother always smiled—with his mouth, his eyes, even the little quirk in his straight brows. Julen once said that he'd been born smiling, and he'd probably die the same. But there was no smile on his wide mouth now.

"Papa?" I asked, my throat suddenly hurting.

He nodded just once. "Wants us both. We'd better be quick."

I batted aside the door hanging and ran out. My bare feet slapped the cold stone flooring, and I shivered and yanked my blanket closer. I felt the old wool give and the hole at my elbow widened as I dashed past the warmth of the kitchen and up the tower stairs.

Bran was just behind me. Neither of us spoke as we toiled round and round, up to the little room at the top of the tallest tower of our castle. The cold was bitter, promising a fierce winter. As I ran

4

I pulled my blanket tighter, tucking the ends through the rope I used as a sash.

The fourth round brought us to Papa's room. To my surprise he was completely alone—the villagers who had taken turns sitting with him had been sent away—and the windows were wide open. Despite two of our three precious Fire Sticks burning brightly in the fireplace and on a makeshift brazier near the bed, the room was shockingly cold.

"Papa—" I cried, flinging myself down by the high, narrow bed. "It's not good for you to be so cold when you're sick—"

"Leave it, child." His voice was just a whisper. "I want to die hearing the windharps. Already the Hill Folk mourn me . . ."

I heard it then, a faint, steady humming on the wintry breeze, carried down from the distant mountain peaks. The sound was eerie but strangely calming, and I turned away from the window, the cold air forgotten.

"Papa—" That was Bran.

Our father's gray beard stirred as he turned his head. He gave Bran a weak, tired smile, no more than a twitching of the lips, and it wrenched at my heart. "Be not sad, my boy. Be pleased," Papa said slowly. "The Hill Folk honor me. All my life I have kept the Covenant, and I shall die keeping it. They know it, and they send their music to guide my spirit from the mortal realm."

I took his hand, which felt cold and dry. Pressing it against my cheek, I said, "But Papa, you are not to worry about Greedy Galdran's tax demand. I've found a way to pay it—I just finished!"

The gnarled fingers briefly gripped my hand. "It's no longer time for taxes, child. It's time to go to war. Galdran's demand was not meant to be fulfilled. It was an excuse. His cousin wants our lands."

"But we're not ready," I protested numbly. "Just one more year—" I heard the scrape of a shoe behind me, and Bran touched my shoulder.

Papa smiled wearily. "Meliara. Branaric and Khesot know the

time is come, but that is what they are trained for. Indeed, daughter, they are ready because of the help you have given them this past year."

I fell silent, and he looked from me to my brother and then back, and then spoke slowly and with increasing difficulty.

"Remember, my children…although your mother chose to adopt into my family, she was a Calahanras…the last of the very finest royal house ever to rule Remalna. If she had wanted, she could have raised her banner, and half the kingdom would have risen, gladly, in her name. You two are half Calahanras. You have her wit, and her brains. You can take Remalna, and you will be better rulers than any Merindar ever was."

I stared at my father, not knowing what to say. To think. It was the first time he had mentioned our mother since that horrible day, nearly ten years ago, when the news had come that she had died so suddenly and mysteriously while on a journey to the capital, Remalna-city.

"Promise me," he said, struggling up on one elbow. His breath wheezed in and out, and his skin was blotchy with the effort, but his voice was strong. "Promise me!…You will…fight Galdran… protect Tlanth…and the Covenant…" He fell back, fought for breath.

"Papa," I quavered.

Beside me, Bran reached for the frail old hand. "Papa, please. Rest. Be easy—"

"*Promise!*" He gripped both our hands, pulling us toward him. "You must…promise me…"

"I promise," I said quickly.

"And I," Branaric said. "Now, Papa, you must try to rest."

"It's too late for…" His eyes closed, and his fingers loosened from mine, and wandered without purpose over the bedclothes. "Khesot…You and Khesot, Branaric…as soon as our hirelings get here from Denlieff, then you attack. Surprise…will carry you a long way."

Bran nodded. "Just as you say, Papa."

"And trust Azmus," Papa said, trembling with the effort it took to speak clearly. "He was your mother's liegeman... If—if he had been with her on that cursed trip, she would be with us now... Listen to him. I didn't, once, and..." Grief wracked his face, grief and pain.

"We understand, Papa," Bran said quickly. I couldn't talk—my throat hurt too much.

Our father gave a long sigh of relief and fell back on his pillows. "You're a good boy, Branaric. No, a man now...a man these four years. And Meliara, almost grown..." He turned his head to look at me. Horror seized my wits when I saw the sheen of tears in his eyes. "Meliara, so like your mother. I wronged you, my daughter. Please forgive me for neglecting you..."

Neglect? I thought of the years that Bran had reluctantly gone up to the tower to wrestle with musty old learning-books while I ran free with Oria and the other village children and, in summers, roamed the high mountains to dance with the Hill Folk under the full moon. My father had always seemed a distant, preoccupied man, and after Mother's death he had become even more distant. It was her I'd missed, and still missed.

Now I sucked in my breath, trying hard not to cry. "But I was happy, Papa," I said. "It wasn't neglect, it was freedom."

My father smiled. The tears shone in the furrows beside his eyes. "Free..." I don't know if he was repeating what I said or beginning a new thought; whichever, it was destined to remain unfinished, at least in this world.

He fell silent, his hands reaching again. This time when we each gripped his fingers, there was no response, and after a moment his breath slowed, then stopped.

Branaric stood helplessly, looking down at the still figure in the bed. Feeling numb—unreal—I took Papa's thin hands, which were still warm, and laid them gently across his breast. Then I turned to my brother. "There's nothing we can do now, except gather the villagers..." *And prepare the funeral fires.* I couldn't say the words.

Bran's chest heaved in a sob, and he pressed the heels of his palms to his eyes. His grief dissolved my numbness, and I began to weep.

Bran opened his arms and I cast myself into them, and we stood there for a long time, crying together while the cold wind swirled round us and the distant windharps of the Hill Folk hummed.

It was Bran who pulled away suddenly. He gripped my shoulders. "Mel, we have to keep that promise. Both of us. But you don't know—" He shook his head and knuckled his eyes. "Together. I know I'm the oldest, and Papa named me the heir, but I promise right now, we'll share the title. Half and half, you and me, even if we disagree—which I hope won't happen. All we have now is this old castle, and the county's people to protect—and each other."

"I don't want to be a countess," I said, sniffling. "Look at me! Wearing a horse blanket and running about with bare feet! I don't know the first thing about being a countess."

"You're not going to Court," Bran said. "You're going to war. And about that"—he winced—"about that, I think you know just about as much as I do."

"What do you mean?"

Bran looked quickly at Papa's body and then said, "I know it's stupid, but I don't feel right about telling you these things up here. Let's stop the fires and go downstairs."

Each of us moved to one of the blazes and said the Words of Power over a Fire Stick. The fires flickered out with a snap. I picked up my Stick, which was still warm; I wrapped my chilled fingers around it and waited as Bran slowly, with a last glance at the still figure on the bed, picked his up.

"Have you been keeping secrets from Papa?" I asked, full of foreboding, as we started down the long spiral.

"Had to." Bran took a deep, unsteady breath. "He aged ten years when Mama was killed, and every year since, he's seemed to add another ten. Until this year. Of late each *day* seems to have added ten."

"Better tell me, then," I said.

"There's no way to make this easy," Bran warned as we reached the ground floor again. "First you should know why Papa wanted us to go on the attack right away: Azmus has proof that the King, and his cousin, plan to break the Covenant. It's a letter that Debegri wrote. It's full of fancy language, but what it means is he's offering our colorwoods for sale outside our kingdom. For gold."

I sucked in a deep breath. "What about the Hill Folk? The woods are theirs! It's been that way for centuries!"

Branaric shook his head slowly. "Not if Debegri gets his way —and Azmus knows the King is behind this scheme, because it was his messengers who were sent to carry the letter."

"But we haven't heard from those warrior captains we hired—"

"Now it's time for you to hear the secret I kept from Papa." Bran looked grim. "Those mercenaries from Denlieff took our money and vanished."

I stopped and faced him. "What? Do we know that for certain? Could they have been delayed—or ambushed—by Galdran?"

Bran shrugged. "I don't know. The only reliable informant we could send to find out would be Azmus."

"But isn't he still in the capital with Papa's letter to the King?"

Branaric nodded. "Awaiting the signal to deliver it and disperse copies through all the Court, just as Papa ordered. But as to the mercenaries from Denlieff, both our messengers have come back and said the commander isn't to be found. No one's even heard of him or his troop." Bran added sourly, "I thought all along this was as risky as trusting skunks not to smell."

I nodded as we stopped by the empty kitchen and laid the Fire Sticks on the great table. "But Papa was so certain they'd believe in our cause."

"Mercenaries don't have causes—or they wouldn't be swords

for hire," Bran said. "We really need someone trained to captain our people and teach us the latest fighting techniques."

"We can't hire anyone else; we haven't the gold," I said. "I just spent two days trying to work around the sums we had to send for the taxes."

Bran raised his hands. "Then we are on our own, sister."

I groaned as we walked the last few steps to the old stewards' parlor, and I swatted aside the hanging. Then I stopped again and groaned louder. I'd forgotten the broken window. All my careful piles of paper were strewn around the room like so much snow.

Bran looked around and scratched his head. "I sure hope you wrote down your figures," he said with a rueful smile.

"Of course I didn't," I muttered.

He slewed around and stared at me. "You didn't?"

"No. I hate writing. It's slow, and my letters are still ill formed, and the ink blobs up, and my fingers get stiff in the cold. I simply separated all the villages' lists of resources and figured out who could give a bit more. Those papers went in one pile. The villages that are overreached went in another pile. I made mental trades in my mind until I managed to match the totals demanded by Galdran. Then I was going to find Oria and tell it all to her so she could write it down." I shrugged.

Though I'd only learned to read and write the year before, it was I who kept track of our careful hoard of supplies, and the taxes, and the plans—and now all my work was scattered over the stone floor of the room.

We both stared until the *plop-plop* of raindrops coming through the broken window and landing on the papers forced us into action.

Working together, we soon got all the papers picked up. Bran silently gave me his stack, and I pressed them all tightly against me. "I still have the totals in my head," I assured him. "I'll find Oria and get her to write it out, and we can see where we are. We'll be all right, Bran. We will." I wanted desperately to see that stricken look leave his eyes—or I would begin crying all over again.

Bran lifted his gaze from the mess of rain-spattered papers in my arms and smiled crookedly. "A horse blanket, Mel?"

I remembered what I was wearing. "It tore in half when Hrani tried washing it. She was going to mend it. This piece was too small for a horse, but it was just right for me."

Bran laughed a little unsteadily. "Mel. A *horse blanket*."

"Well, it's clean," I said defensively. "Was—at least, it doesn't smell of horse."

Bran sank down onto the three-legged stool, still laughing; but it was a strange, wheezy sort of laugh. "A countess wearing a horse blanket and a count who hates fighting, leading a war against a wicked king who has the largest army the kingdom has ever known. What's to become of us, Mel?"

I knelt down—carefully, because of the broken crockery—set my papers aside, and took his hands. "One thing I've learned about doing the figures: You don't look at the problem all at once, or it's like being caught in a spring flood under a downpour. You tackle the problem in pieces...We'll send our letter to the King. Maybe Galdran will actually listen, and abide by the Covenant, and ease taxes, so we don't have to go to war. But if he doesn't, some of those courtiers ought to agree with us—they can't all be Galdran's toadies—which means we'll surely get allies. Then we'll gather the last of our supplies. And then..."

"And then?" Bran repeated, his hands on his knees, his dark blue eyes even darker with the intensity of his emotions.

"And then..." I faltered, feeling overwhelmed with my own emotions. I took a deep breath, reminding myself of my own advice. *Pieces. Break it all into small pieces.* "And then, if Galdran attacks us, we'll fight back. Like I said, maybe we'll have help. The courtiers will see it in Papa's letter to the King: We are not doing this for ourselves. We're doing it to protect the Hill Folk, for if Papa is right, and Galdran's cousin wants to break the Covenant and start chopping down the great trees again, then the Hill Folk will have nowhere to live. *And* we're doing it for our people—though not just them. For all the people in the kingdom who've had to pay those harsh taxes in order to build Galdran that big army."

Branaric got to his feet. "You're right. In pieces. I'll remember that...Let's get through today first. We have to tell everyone in the village about Papa, and send messengers throughout Tlanth, and get ready for the funeral fire."

My first impulse was to run and hide, for I did not look forward to facing all that pity. But it had to be done—and we had to do it together.

And afterward, when the village was quiet and lights went out, I could slip out of the castle and run up the mountainside to where I could hear the reed flutes mourning.

The Hill Folk would emerge, looking a little like walking trees in the moons' light, and wordlessly, accompanied by their strange music—which was a kind of magic in itself—we would dance slowly, sharing memory, and grief, and promise.

TWO

IT WAS EXACTLY A MONTH LATER THAT JULEN, ORIA, Hrani the weaver, and I gathered in the kitchen—the only warm room in the castle—and studied Bran from all angles.

He flushed with embarrassment but turned around willingly enough while we judged the fit of the tunic Hrani had remade for him. The old green velvet, left from Papa's wardrobe, nicely set off Bran's tall, rangy build. His face was long and sharp boned, like Father's had been.

The only features Bran and I shared were wide-spaced dark blue eyes and wavy red-brown hair—both inherited from our mother. The green of the tunic was just right for his coloring.

"This tunic might not be the fashion—" Julen began.

"Of course it's not the fashion," Oria cut in, her dark eyes full of scorn for the vagaries of courtiers. "When from all accounts their fashions change from week to week—maybe day to day."

"This tunic might not be the fashion," her mother repeated as if Oria had not spoken, "but it looks good. And wear your hair tied back, not loose or braided. Better stay with the simple styles than look foolish in what might be old styles."

Bran shrugged. He had as little interest in clothing as I did. "As long as they don't take one look and laugh me back into the snow, I'm content." He turned to me and sighed. "But I can't help wishing you were going. You've a much quicker mind than I have."

Quick to laugh, quick to act—and much too quick to judge. How many times had I heard that warning? I stole a look at Julen, who pursed her lips but said nothing.

I shook my head. "No, no, you got all the charm in this family—along with the imposing height. All I got was the temper. This is a mission to win allies, not enemies, and if they laughed *me* back into the snow, you *know* I'd go right back at them, sword in hand, and try to make them listen!"

Bran and Oria laughed, and even Julen smiled. I crossed my arms. "You know it's true."

"Of course," Bran agreed. "That's why it's funny. I can just see you taking on a palace full of sniffy courtiers twice your size, as if they were a pack of unruly pups—"

"Here, my lord, try the blue one now," Julen said. Despite the title—which she had insisted on using since Father's death—her tone was very much like the one she reserved for little Calaub and his urchin friends. "And that's enough nonsense. You'll do well if you go down to those barons and talk like you mean it. And you, my lady," she rounded on me, "if you wish to be helpful, you can see if Selfan has finished resoling the blackweave boots."

I got up, knowing a dismissal when I heard one.

Oria started after me but paused at the door, looking back, a considering expression on her pretty face. I looked as well, but I saw only Bran unlacing his tunic as he talked to Julen about those boots.

Oria gave a tiny shrug and pushed me out the door.

"Something wrong?" I asked.

Her dark eyes gleamed with humor now. "Mama is very cross, isn't she? I don't think she wants your brother going to the low-lands."

It was not quite an answer, but during the last couple of years I'd gotten used to Oria's occasional mysterious evasions. "Can't be

14

helped. Azmus wrote out copies of our letter to the King and gave them to prominent courtiers, but not one response have we received. It's time to get some allies with face-to-face meetings, or we're finished before we even start."

She pursed her lips, the humor gone. "I made him up some good things to eat," she said. "Let me fetch the pack."

Not too much later we all stood in the castle courtyard as Branaric finished tying his travel gear onto the saddle of his horse. Then he mounted, gave us a quick salute, and soon was gone from sight.

He didn't like saying farewells any more than I did. I retreated back into the castle, and for a time wandered from room to empty room as cold drafts of wintry wind chilled my face. Inevitably my path brought me to the library, empty these ten years. Black scorch marks still stained the walls and ceiling, potent reminders of the terrible night we found out about my mother's death. Crying in rage, my father had stamped into this room, where generations of Astiars had stored their gathered knowledge, and deliberately—one book at a time—set it all ablaze. The only books that had escaped were a half dozen dull tomes in the schoolroom.

After, Father had retreated to his tower, and never again referred to that night. But his determination to see Galdran toppled from the throne had altered from desire to obsession.

I paced the perimeter of the room, looking at the grimy ash-blackened stones, my mood dark.

Oria's voice broke my reverie: "Amazing, isn't it, how one can live in a mess and never really notice it? Perhaps we ought to scour these rooms out come spring."

I turned around. Oria stood in the open doorway—the hanging had rotted entirely away a few years back. "Why? The weather will just blow more leaves in, and we can't afford windows."

"The wind won't blow ten years' worth in at once," Oria said practically.

I looked around, wondering why I resisted the idea. Was this room a kind of monument? Except I knew my mother would not have liked a burnt, blackened room as a memorial. In her day, the furnishings might have been old and worn, for taxes even then had been fierce, but each table and cushion and candlestick had been mended and polished, and the castle had been cozy and clean and full of flowers. And this room . . .

"She loved books," I said slowly. "It was Papa who declared war on them, just as he did on Galdran. I really don't know why Papa burned this room. Nor do I know how to find out." I reached a decision. "Maybe we should clean it. Except—what a chore!"

Oria grinned. "A challenge. I've wanted to set this castle to rights for—" She stopped suddenly and shook her head. "Mama said to bring you down to the smithy. You can sleep in the loft. That way we can add this Fire Stick to the two we've already put in our supply pack."

I nodded, glad to be relieved of having to sleep alone in the castle. It wasn't the sadness of the past lingering in shadowy corners that bothered me so much as my own fears about the future.

During the long, snowbound month that followed, I kept busy. The few times I had nothing to do, Julen assigned me chores. She called herself my maid, and her directions were framed in the form of a question ("Would you care to deliver these mended halters to the garrison, my lady?"), but otherwise she treated me much as she treated Oria. I found this comforting. I didn't feel so much like an orphan.

We spent a lot of time at the old garrison—a leftover from the days when every noble had some kind of private army—training in swordfighting with all those who had volunteered to help in the war. Our army was comprised mostly of young people from villages across Tlanth.

In charge now was Khesot, a man whose seventy years had been

devoted to the service of the Counts and Countesses of Tlanth—
our father, and his grandmother before him—except for a five-year
stint fighting for the old King during the long siege when the in-
famous pirate fleet called the Brotherhood of Blood had tried to
gain access to the coastal cities. It was these five years' service as a
soldier that had gotten him placed in the position he was in now.
He'd never risen higher than leader of a riding, but he knew enough
of war to realize his own shortcomings. And he was the best we
had.

The huge, drafty building echoed with the clanks and thuds
and shouts of mock battle. Khesot walked slowly up and back, his
mild brown eyes narrowed, considering, as he watched us work.

"Get that shield arm up," he said to a tough old stonemason.
"Remember you will likely be fighting mounted warriors, and I very
much fear that most of us will be afoot. The mounted fighter has
the advantage; therefore you must unhorse your opponent before
you can hope to win..."

We had spent days affixing shiny metal bits to our shields to
reflect sunlight at the horses and cause them to rear. We had also
practiced slicing saddle belts, hooking spears or swords around legs
and heaving warriors out of the saddle. And we learned other meth-
ods of unhorsing warriors, such as tying fine-woven twine between
two trees at just the right height so that the riders would be knocked
off their horses.

Khesot turned around, then frowned at two young men who
had assumed the old dueling stance and were slashing away at one
another with merry abandon, their swords ringing.

"Charic! Justav! What do you think you are doing?"

The men stopped, Charic looking shamefaced. "Thought we'd
refine a little, in case we take on one o' them aristos—"

"Many of whom are trained in swordplay from the time they
begin to walk," Khesot cut in, his manner still mild; but now both
young men had red faces. "By the very best sword masters their
wealthy parents can hire. It would take them precisely as long as it

17

amused them to cut you to ribbons. Do not engage their officers in a duel, no matter how stupid you might think them. Two of you, moving as I told you, can knock them off balance . . ."

He went on to lecture the two, who listened soberly. Several others gathered around to listen as well.

Oria and I had been working with one another until I stopped to watch. Now Oria lowered her sword arm and eyed me. "What's wrong?"

I dropped my point, absently massaging my shoulder. "Did I frown? I was—well, thinking of something."

She shrugged, and we went back to practice. But I kept part of my attention on Khesot, and when he drew near to us, I disengaged and said, "I have a question for you."

Khesot nodded politely, and as we walked to the side of the room, he said, "May I compliment you, my lady, on your improvement?"

"You may," I said grimly, "but I know I'm still not good enough to face anyone but a half-trained ten-year-old."

He smiled. "You cannot help your stature."

"You mean I'm short and scrawny, and I'll always be short and scrawny, and short and scrawny makes for a terrible warrior."

His smile widened; for a moment he was on the verge of laughter. As he positioned himself so he could continue to watch the practice, he said, "You have a question for me?"

"Something I've been worrying about; what you told Charic and Justav put me in mind of it. Even if we have the best-trained warriors in the world, how can we really hope to defeat that army of Galdran's? I can see how long it takes to beat just one person, and you know that even Faeruk, who is our best, won't be able to take on whole ridings."

"I am hoping that the most the King will send against us will be a couple of wings," Khesot said. "Twice-nine ridings, with their foot soldiers, we can probably handle, if we plan well and use our familiarity with the territory to our advantage."

"Well," I said, "I was thinking: Instead of having to do all this hacking and slashing, could it be possible to try other means to defeat them—through discouragement or even dismay?"

"What have you in mind?"

"It is the King's cousin, Baron Debegri, who wants our lands," I said. "Rumor has it he is a pompous fool. If we were to make him look foolish, might he give it up as a bad business and go home?" Khesot was silent, so I continued, outlining my plans. "Supposing we could, oh, turn aside a stream uphill from their camp and swamp them in their bedrolls. Or sneak in and add pepper to their food. Or sit in trees and drop powdered itchwort on them as they ride beneath."

Khesot paused, his eyes distant. Finally he turned to me, his expression curious, and said, "Who is to execute these admirable plans?"

"I will," I said immediately. "I know I'm never going to be much good in these hand-to-hand battles, but climbing trees is something I can do better than most. I'll ask for volunteers. I know Oria will join me, and Young Varil. Old Varil says he's too small to handle a sword, and he wants so badly to help. And—"

Khesot lifted a hand. "I had not considered that you would actually go into battle with us, my lady. I thought your practice here was mostly for diversion."

I felt my face go hot. "I guess that's a polite way of telling me that I really *am* bad with the sword, then?"

He smiled a little. "No, it's just that members of the nobility don't usually lead battles unless they've been trained their whole lives."

"But I will never ask anyone from our village—from any village in Tlanth—to risk his or her life unless I'm willing to myself."

"You must realize, my lady, if Galdran's people catch you, they will treat you like any other prisoner..."

"We're all equally at risk," I said. "But my plan is to be sneaky, so they are surprised."

He bowed. "Then I leave it to you, my lady."

I bowed back. "I'll get started right away!"

Though I still missed my brother and worried because he sent no message, having a plan to work on made the wintry days move faster. I was very busy, often from the first ring of the gold-candle bell at dawn to the single toll of midnight, when those who kept night watches lit the first white candle.

I had a group of five, all younger than Oria and I. We left the good fighters to the ridings, which Khesot was pulling together slowly, as he evaluated the best leaders.

It being midwinter, herbs were hard to come by, but assiduous poking into ancient grottoes seldom touched by the weather, and patient communication through friends and relatives, uncovered some surprising stores. Thus by Midwinter's Day, which was also Oria's Name Day, I had laid by a good supply of itchwort and sneezeweed and three kinds of pepper, plus a collection of other oddments.

Thus I was in a happy mood when I put on a gown that Oria had outgrown and walked out with her to the village square to begin the celebration. For it wasn't just her Name Day, but also her Flower Day; though she'd been doing the women's dances for several years, after today she would no longer dance the children's dances. Young men and women who passed their Flower Days were considered of an age to marry.

A heavy snow over the previous two days had trapped those who might otherwise have gone home to celebrate Midwinter with their families, so we had a larger group than usual. The stars overhead were stunningly clear, as only winter skies can make them. Our breath puffed white as we formed up circles, and some shivered; but we knew we'd soon be warm enough as the musicians began thrumming and tapping a merry tune.

Everyone looked our way. Oria stepped back, smiling, and I

lifted the deep blue cheli blossoms I'd found in one of those old protected grottoes, and tossed them high in the air. They fluttered down around her. She twirled about, her curly black hair brushing against her crimson sash. Then, slowly, stepping to the music, she walked between the two great blazes in the square made by everyone bringing their Fire Sticks. And all her friends flung flowers.

Sometimes she bent to pick them up. Not any special ones, that is, from any special person. She hadn't been twoing with anyone, even though she could have been anytime these past three years. As I watched her deft fingers twist the stems of the blossoms into a garland, I felt a kind of swooping sensation inside when I realized that we *both* had been of the age to be twoing with the young men for three years.

My Flower Day was coming up in just weeks. My Flower Day—and I was still happiest dancing with the children.

But there was no time to consider this. The circle walk ended, and Oria carefully placed her garland on her head, then held out her hands to me. "Come, Mel, let's dance!"

We moved into the cleared space, which was now dappled with blossoms in a kind of mirror to the brightly colored jewels in the sky. Warmth radiated from the fires, and soon we were flushed from the dance.

Before the young men could move out for their own first dance, the sound of horses' hooves approaching made the musicians falter. Memory of imminent war, forgotten for a short time, now rushed back on us. I could see it in the quick looks, the hands that strayed to knife hilts or stooped for rocks.

A horse and rider emerged from the shadows into our silence. I watched in surprise as my brother rode directly up to us, and just behind him a small, round-faced man on another horse—Azmus.

Bran's mount halted in the center of our dance square, its limbs trembling, and my brother slid off, almost pitching forward. Several people sprang forward to help, some to hold him up, others to take the horse away to be cared for. Behind, Azmus dismounted, and though he didn't lose his balance, his face was haggard. His horse was also led away.

I ran to Branaric and stared with dismay into his drawn face. His hair had come loose and hung in wet strings across his brow and down over his soggy cloak. He opened his mouth, but no words came out.

Her garland askew, Oria handed Branaric a steaming cloth. He buried his face and hands gratefully in it for a long moment. The only sound in the square was the crackling of the flames.

Finally he looked up, his skin blotchy but his eyes clearing. "War," he said, and cleared his throat. "Azmus found out, and came to get me. The King has sent his cousin to take Tlanth for non-payment of taxes. And for conspiring to break the Covenant."

THREE

GALDRAN HAD TWO FORTRESSES ON THE BORDER OF Tlanth, one to the south, called Vesingrui, and a smaller one on our northeast border, called Munth. This castle was much closer to the wealthy and powerful and somewhat mysterious principality of Renselaeus—about whose leaders we knew little, other than that they were allied with Galdran.

It was the castle of Munth that would see the start of the war. Munth was closest to our castle and the heart of Tlanth. If Munth were kept well supplied, Galdran's forces would find it the easier to settle in all winter and throw warriors against us.

Some of the younger people wanted to attack Vesingrui first, for that would be more daring, it being closest to the lowlands. But Khesot wisely pointed out that we couldn't actually hold it; we'd be divided in half, and a small army divided into two tiny forces wouldn't be much good for anything.

So two days after Oria's Flower Day, just ahead of a terrible snowstorm, Azmus rode south to return to Remalna-city for spying purposes while the rest of us marched down the mountains to Munth. We found it nearly empty, though the soldiers there were obviously preparing for more inhabitants. We surprised them in the midst of a huge cleanup.

The fight was short, and soon Galdran's people were locked in their own dungeon. The storm struck while we were snug in the castle.

While our army celebrated its first victory, Khesot called Bran and me and our riding leaders together. The echoes of happy songs rang off the mossy ancient stones as we met in the high round room set aside for the commander. Outside the wind howled, and the thick windows showed pure white. But we lit one of our own castle's Fire Sticks and huddled around it, drinking hot cider, until the room had lost some of its chill.

On a huge wood table was spread the map I'd carefully made the summer before. It showed all of Tlanth, every village, every mountain, and all the rivers and valleys I knew so well.

"Debegri is on his way here," Khesot said finally, gesturing with his pipe at the map. "None of our prisoners would tell us when they received their orders, but I suspect, from the evidence around us, he and his warriors are expected imminently."

"Good!" Bran said, laughing as he brandished his cider cup. "So what's next? A welcome party?"

"A welcome party of ghosts, I think," Khesot said. "We don't know how many Debegri is leading, and we don't have enough supplies to outlast a siege. I wish our timing had been better—before the army but after their supplies got here. Then we could have held out indefinitely."

"Except they could have penned us here and attacked the rest of Tlanth, couldn't they?" I asked doubtfully.

"Exactly, my lady," Khesot said, giving me a thin smile of approval. "Whatever forces they have are probably hunkered down somewhere, waiting out this storm. No one's going anywhere until it ends. Therefore what I suggest is that we use the time the storm lasts to completely destroy this castle. Render it unusable for them, forcing them to carry their supplies with them—at least for the time being."

"And we can pick away at them, getting some of those supplies," Old Varil said grimly.

"And keep them away from our villages, so they can't set up bases there," Hrani added, tucking her shawl around her more tightly as an especially fierce gust of wind sent a trickle of icy air stirring through the room.

"But that's defensive work," I protested. "Aren't we going to go on the attack?"

Khesot puffed at his pipe and nodded at me. "The time has come to ignore all the rhetoric. We call this war a revolt. They call us traitors. The truth is, Galdran has attacked us here in our homeland, and we have to defend it."

"At least until we get some allies," Branaric said, still smiling. "They're all afraid of Galdran, every single person I spoke with. Take Gharivar of Mnend—he's right below us, and if Debegri wants more land, Mnend will be next. I may not be as quick at understanding hints as Mel, but I could see he agreed with me, even though he didn't dare promise anything. Orbanith listened as well. And a couple of the coastal barons."

Khesot frowned slightly but just puffed away at his pipe without speaking. It was then that I began to believe that we were going to have to fight this one all alone.

We worked for the four days of that blizzard, loosening the mortar in the lower stones of Castle Munth. The wind and storm did the rest; after the walls fell, we melted snow from uphill with our combined Fire Sticks. The resulting flood was impressive.

By the next morning, when the scouts we left behind saw the first of Debegri's soldiers march up the road, the whole mess had frozen into ice, with our ex-prisoners wandering around poking dismally at the ruins. It would take a great deal of effort to make any use of Munth, and the scouts were still laughing when they came to report.

———

For five whole weeks, this was how it went.

We froze the roads ahead of Debegri's marching warriors. We changed road signs, removed landmarks, used snow to alter the landscape. Three times we sat on the cliffs above and cracked jokes while the army milled around in confusion far below us.

We attacked their camps at night, flinging snow and stones at those on the perimeter and then disappearing into the woods before the angry Baron could assemble a retaliation party.

The only one we couldn't get at was Debegri, for he had a splendid—even palatial—tent that was closely guarded in the very center of their camp. He also had lancers riding in double columns on either side of him whenever his army moved.

But we actually did get to use the itchwort.

As soon as I saw Galdran's army I realized it would be impossible to drop itchwort on them, for they were much better bundled up than we were. Steel helms, thick cloaks, chain mail, thick gauntlets, long battle tunics—brown and green, dark versions of the gold and green of Remalna—and high blackweave boots kept everything covered. In disappointment I'd told my little band to put the packets of itchwort at the bottoms of our carryalls.

But one night, after we'd flooded their camp by blocking up a stream just above them, the chance came. The weather was ugly, slashing sleet and stinging rain rendering the world soggy. Debegri, always recognizable in his embroidered gold cloak and the white-plumed helm of a commander, stalked out through a line of torch bearers and waved his arms, yelling.

Half of his army marched off into the darkness, presumably in search of us. The rest labored to strike the camp. Varil, Oria, and I perched high in trees, watching. At one point something happened at the other end of the camp, and for a short time Debegri's mighty tent lay collapsed and half rolled on its ground cover.

I looked over at Oria. "Itchwort," I murmured.

Varil snorted into the crook of his elbow so the sound wouldn't carry.

"I don't know," Oria whispered doubtfully. "Those sentries may come marching back just as quickly..."

"You stay and watch," I whispered back. "Give the crow call if you see danger. Varil, we'll have to crawl through mud—"

Varil was already digging through his pack.

We scrambled down from our tree and elbow-crawled our way through the mud to the partially folded tent. There both of us emptied our packs into it and scattered the dust as best we could, then we retreated—and just in time. The tent was soon packed up, loaded onto its dray.

When Debegri camped again, we were lined up in the rocks of a cliff to the east, watching eagerly. To our vast disappointment, he didn't emerge at all—for three days.

For the week after that he had almost the entire army guarding him, which made it easy to harass their sentries. And one night we managed to steal half their horse picket.

That was the last and most triumphant of our exploits; we celebrated long past midnight, sure that if the war was going to be like this, we'd win before the spring thaws came to the mountains.

We celebrated too soon.

The next time Debegri sent a wing after us, they broke the Code of War and used arrows. Debegri had archers with him, probably hired from another land. Three of our people were hit, and from then on we were forced to stay under the cover of forestland.

And so for a time we were at an impasse; they did not advance, but we were more cautious about attacking. They had broken the Code of War, but we had no one to complain to. Against my wishes, Branaric sent some of our people to find bows and arrows, and to learn how to shoot them.

Then the day came when a new column was spotted riding up behind Debegri's force. We almost missed them, for we had also begun staying in a tight group. But luckily Khesot, cautious since his days in the terrible Pirate Wars, still sent pairs of scouts on rounds in all four directions twice a day.

It was Seliar, of my group, who spotted them first. She reported to me, and the rest of us crept down the hillside to watch the camp below. We saw at the head of the column a man wearing a long black cloak.

Debegri emerged, bowed. The newcomer bowed in return and handed the Baron a rolled paper. They went inside Debegri's tent, and when they emerged, the stranger had the white plume of leadership on his helm. Debegri's glower was plain even at the distance we watched from.

Backing up from our vantage, we retreated to our camp.

Bran and Khesot and the other riding leaders were all gathered under our old, patched rain cover when we reached them. Seliar blurted out what we'd seen.

Branaric grinned all through the story. At the end I said, "This is obviously no surprise. What news had you?"

Bran nodded to where a mud-covered young woman sat in front of one of the tents, attacking a bowl of stew as if she hadn't eaten in a week. "Messenger just arrived from Azmus, or it would have been a surprise. Galdran has taken his cousin off the command. He'd apparently expected us to last two weeks at most."

"Well, who is this new commander? Ought we to be afraid?"

Bran's grin widened until he laughed. "Here's the jest: He's none other than the Marquis of Shevraeth, heir to the Renselaeus principality. According to Azmus, all he ever thinks about are clothes, horse racing, and gambling. And did I mention clothes?"

Everyone roared with laughter.

"We'll give *him* two weeks," I crowed. "And then we'll send him scurrying back to his tailor."

FOUR

IT TOOK ONE LONG, DESPERATE WEEK TO PROVE JUST how wrong was my prophecy.

"The revolution is not over," Branaric said seriously some ten days later.

But even this—after a long, horrible day of real fighting, a desperate run back into the familiar hills of Tlanth, and the advent of rain beating on the tent over our heads—failed to keep Branaric serious for long. His mouth curved wryly as he added, "And today's action was not a rout, it was a retreat."

"So we will say outside this tent." Khesot paused to tap his pipeweed more deeply into the worn brown bowl of his pipe, then he looked up, his white eyebrows quirked. "But it *was* a rout."

I said indignantly, "Our people fought well!"

Khesot gave a stately, measured nod in my direction, without moving from his cushion. "Valiantly, Lady Meliara, valiantly. But courage is not enough when we are so grossly outnumbered. More so now that they have an equally able commander."

Bran sighed. "Why haven't we heard anything from Gharivar of Mnend, or Chamadis from Turlee, on the border? I *know* they both hate Galdran as much as we do, and they as much as promised to help."

"Perhaps they have been cut off from joining us, Lord Branaric," Khesot said, nodding politely this time to Bran.

"Cut off by cowardice," I muttered. My clothes were clammy, my skin cold; I longed to change into my one other outfit, but we had to finish our own war council before facing the riding leaders. So I perched on the hard camp cushion, arms clasped tightly around my legs.

Bran turned to me, frowning. "You think they lied to me, then?"

"I just think you're better off not counting on those Court fools. Remember, Papa always said they are experts at lying with a smile, and their treaties don't last as long as the wine haze after the signing."

Bran's eyes went serious again under his straight brows. "I know, Mel," he said, plainly unhappy as he picked absently at a threadbare patch on his cushion. "But if we don't get help . . . Well, we're just not enough."

Leaving us staring at the grinning skull of defeat. I shook my head, shivering when my wet clothes shifted on my back and sent a chill down my flesh. Now Bran looked worn, tired—and defeated—and I was angry with myself for having spoken. "Khesot has the right of it," I said. "Perhaps they really were cut off."

I looked up, caught a glance of approval in Khesot's mild brown eyes. Heartened, I said, "Look. We aren't lying to our people when we say this is a retreat. Because even if we *have* been routed, we're still in our own territory, hills we know better than anyone. Meanwhile we've evaded Greedy Galdran's mighty army nearly all winter. A long time! Didn't Azmus say Galdran promised the Court our heads on poles after two days?"

"So Debegri swore," Bran said, smiling a little.

"That means we've held out all these weeks despite the enormous odds against us, and word of this has to be reaching the rest of the kingdom. Maybe those eastern Counts will decide to join us—and some of the other grass-backed vacillators as well," I finished stoutly.

Bran grinned. "Maybe so," he said. "And you're right. The higher Shevraeth drives us, the more familiar the territory. If we plan aright, we can lead them on a fine shadow chase and pick them off as they run. Maybe more traps..."

Khesot's lips compressed, and I shivered again. "More traps? You've already put out a dozen. Bran, I really hate those things."

Branaric winced, then he shook his head, his jaw tightening. "This is war. Baron Debegri was the first to start using arrows, despite the Code of War, and now Shevraeth has got us cut off from our own castle—and our supplies. We have to use every weapon to hand, and if that means planting traps for their unwary feet, so be it."

I sighed. "It is so...dishonorable. We have outlawed the use of traps against animals for over a century. And what if the Hill Folk stumble onto one?"

"I told you last week," Bran said, "my first command to those placing the traps is to lay sprigs of stingflower somewhere nearby. The Hill Folk won't miss those. Their noses will warn them to tread lightly long before their eyes will."

"We are also using arrows," I reminded him. "So that's two stains on our honor."

"But we are vastly outnumbered. Some say thirty to one."

I looked up at Khesot. "What think you?"

The old man puffed his pipe alight. The red glow in the bowl looked warm and welcome as pungent smoke drifted through the tent. Then he lowered the pipe and said, "I don't like them, either. But I like less the thought that this Marquis is playing with us, and anytime he wishes he could send his force against us and smash us in one run. He has to know pretty well where we are."

"At least you can make certain you keep mapping those traps, so our folk don't stumble into them," I said, giving in.

"That I promise. They'll be marked within a day of being set," Branaric said.

Neither Branaric nor Khesot displayed any triumph as Branaric reached for and carefully picked up the woven tube holding our

31

precious map. Branaric's face was always easy to read—as easy as my own—and though Khesot was better at hiding his emotions, he wasn't perfect. They did not like using the traps, either, but had hardened themselves to the necessity.

I sighed. Another effect of the war. *I've been raised to this almost my entire life. Why does my spirit fight so against it?*

I thrust away the nagging worries, and the dissatisfactions, and my own physical discomfort, as Bran's patient fingers spread out my map on the rug between us. I focused on its neatly drawn hills and forests, dimly lit by the glowglobe, and tried hard to clear my mind of any thoughts save planning our next action.

But it was difficult. I was worried about our single glowglobe, whose power was diminishing. With our supplies nearly gone and our funds even lower, we no longer had access to the magic wares of the west, so there was no way to obtain new glowglobes.

Khesot was looking not at the map but at us, his old eyes sad.

I winced, knowing what he'd say if asked: that he had not been trained for his position any more than nature had suited Bran and me for war.

But there was no other choice.

"So if Hrani takes her riding up here on Mount Elios, mayhap they can spy out Galdran's numbers better," Branaric said slowly. "Then we send out someone to lure 'em to the Ghost Fall Ravine."

I forced my attention back to the map. "Even if the Marquis fails to see so obvious a trap," I said, finally, smoothing a wrinkle with my fingers, "they're necessarily all strung out going through that bottleneck. I don't see how we can account for many of them before they figure out what we're at, and retreat. I say we strike fast, in total surprise. We could set fire to their tents and steal all their mounts. That'd set 'em back a little."

Bran frowned. "None of our attempts to scare 'em off have worked, though—even with Debegri. He just sent for more reinforcements, and now there's this new commander. Attacking their camp sounds more risky to us than to them."

Khesot still said nothing, leaning over only to tap out and re-load his pipe. I followed the direction of his gaze to my brother's face. Had Branaric been born without title or parental plans, he probably would have found his way into a band of traveling players and there enjoyed a life's contentment. Did one not know him by sight, there was no sign in his worn dress or in his manner that he was a count—and this was even more true for me. I looked at Khesot and wondered if he felt sad that though today was my Flower Day there would be no dancing—no music, or laughter, or family to celebrate the leaving of childhood behind. Among the aristocrats in the lowlands, Flower Day was celebrated with fine dresses and satin slippers and expensive gifts. Did he pity us?

He couldn't understand that I had no regrets for something I'd never known—and believed I never would know. But I controlled my impatience, and my tongue, because I knew from long experience that he was again seeing our mother in us—in our wide, dark-lashed eyes and auburn hair—and she had dearly loved pretty clothing, music, her rose garden.

And Galdran had had her killed.

"What do you think?" Bran addressed Khesot, who smiled ruefully.

"You'll pardon an old man, my lord, my lady. I'm more tired than I thought. My mind wandered and I did not hear what you asked."

"Can you second-guess this Shevraeth?" Branaric asked. "He seems to be driving us back into our hills—to what purpose? Why hasn't he taken over any of our villages? He knows where they lie —and he has the forces. If he does that, traps or no traps, arrows or no arrows, we're lost. We won't be able to retake them."

Khesot puffed again, watching smoke curl lazily toward the tent roof.

In my mind I saw, clearly, that straight-backed figure on the dapple-gray horse, his long black cloak slung back over the animal's haunches, his plumed helm of command on his head. With either phenomenal courage or outright arrogance he had ignored the possibility of our arrows, the crowned sun stitched on his tunic gleaming in the noonday light as he directed the day's battle.

"I do not know," Khesot said slowly. "But judging from our constant retreats of the last week, I confess freely, I do not believe him to be stupid."

I said, "I find it impossible to believe that a Court fop—really, Azmus reported gossip in Remalna claiming him to be the most brainless dandy of them all—could suddenly become so great a leader."

Khesot tapped his pipe again. "Hard to say. Certainly Galdran's famed army did poorly enough against us until he came. But maybe he has good captains, and unlike Debegri, he may listen to them. *They* cannot all be stupid," Khesot said. "They've been guarding the coast and keeping peace in the cities all these years. It could also be they learned from those first weeks' losses to us. They certainly respect us a deal more than they did at the outset." He closed his eyes.

"Which is why I say we ought to attack them at their camp." I jabbed a finger at the map. "There are too many of them to carry their own water. They'll have to camp by a stream, right? Oh, I suppose it isn't realistic, but how I love the image of us setting fire to their tents, and them swarming about like angry ants while we laugh our way back into the hills."

Branaric's ready grin lightened his somber expression. He started to say something, then was taken by a sudden, fierce yawn. Almost immediately my own mouth opened in a jaw-cracking yawn that made my eyes sting.

"We can discuss our alternatives with the riding leaders after we eat, if I may suggest, my lord, my lady," Khesot said, looking anxiously from one of us to the other. "Let me send Saluen to the cook tent for something hot."

Khesot rose and moved to the flap of the tent to look out. He made a sign to the young man standing guard under the rain canopy a short distance away. Saluen came, Khesot gave his order, and we all watched Saluen lope down the trail to the cook tent.

Khesot stayed on his feet, beckoning to my brother. With careful fingers I rolled up our map. I was peripherally aware of the other two talking in low voices, until Branaric confronted me with surprise and consternation plain on his face.

Branaric waited until I had stowed the map away, then he grabbed me in a sudden, fierce hug. "Next year," he said in a husky voice. "Can't make much of your Flower Day, but next year I promise you'll have a Name Day celebration to be remembered forever—and it'll be in the capital!"

"With us as winners, right?" I said, laughing. "It's all right, Bran. I don't think I'm ready for Flower Day yet, anyway. Maybe being so short has made me age slower, or something. I'll be just as happy dancing with the children another year."

Bran smiled back, then turned away and resumed his quiet conversation with Khesot. I listened for a moment to the murmur of their voices and looked at but didn't really notice the steady rain, or the faintly glowing tents.

Instead my inner eye kept returning to the memory of our people running before a mass of orderly brown-and-green-clad soldiers, overseen by a straight figure in a black cloak riding back and forth along a high ridge.

FIVE

AFTER A HASTY SUPPER I SAT IN THE BIG TENT WE'D
fashioned from three smaller ones and looked at each tired, worried face in the circle of riding leaders, and made a private res-
olution.

The truth was, the riding leaders were afraid to attack the
Galdran camp. I didn't blame them. Each had a turn to speak.
Some were hesitant, some apologetic. They didn't sound like warriors, but simply like exhausted men and women. Calaub: a blacksmith by trade, brother to Julen. Hrani: a weaver. Moraun: a miller.
Faeruk: wounded thirty years before, when fighting pirates for the
old King. Only Jusar favored the idea, but he was a rarity: a young
man trained in arms, though for defense of the castle, not for the
field.

And even Jusar seemed tense, voicing his worry that trying to
locate the enemy's main camp might bring trouble down on us.
"They'll surely have more sentries watching than we can find," he
said.

"More sentries than we have warriors," Faeruk joked, and the
others laughed uneasily.

"Who knows? Galdran might even have managed to hire some
magician. For that matter, how did they get so many Fire Sticks?"

Hrani said. Her voice held a little of her old spirit, but there was a stricken expression in her eyes that I could not account for.

"One person in each riding took his or her family's Sticks," Jusar said. "Heard rumors about what is required of new recruits: Obey or die."

Calaub's heavy brows met over his big nose. "Makes sense. Galdran's not going to care about Fire Stick custom—not if he's breaking the Covenant."

"Or trying to," Khesot said with a faint smile, bringing the subject back. "So let's use our alternate plan. Tomorrow, if this weather clears, we can sort out the details."

I stayed quiet as the war council wound up. Then I followed as they filed down the trail to the cook tent to get their evening dose of the thick soup that was tasting each day more of ground corn and stale vegetables and less of stock and herbs.

What we need is information, I thought. *And no one wants to send anyone on what might be a suicide mission, to spy out their camp.* The problem was, we had only one good spy—Azmus. And he was in the capital trying to garner fresh news.

During Debegri's command we'd used some of the older children as horse tenders and arms bearers, but only in isolated places. Some of these youths had willingly climbed very tall trees to survey and report on distant movements. Now, with Shevraeth in command, no one wanted to send a child into direct danger.

Staring upward through a tangle of branches at the glowering ranks of rain clouds, I saw a break, just for a moment. If the latest storm lifted that night, I decided to do the job myself.

As the last of the light disappeared, the showers diminished, and early stars glimmered between the silent clouds moving southward. Wind whipped through the camp, drumming the tent walls. I moved toward my tent, thinking that if I really were to go spying that night, I'd better get to sleep early.

Just before I reached the tent I heard a giggle, sharply broken off. I lifted the flap—and gasped.

Oria stood there grinning, her dark eyes crinkled. All around my little tent were flowers, early spring blooms of every color, some of them from peaks a long ride away. The air was sweet with their combined scents.

"Everybody brought one," she said. "I know it doesn't make up for no music and no dancing, but...Well, it was my idea. Do you like it?"

"It's wonderful." I sniffed happily at a silvery spray of starliss.

"Sit down, Mel," Oria said. "Forget the war, just for a bit. I'll brush out your hair for you."

With a sigh of relief I untucked the end of my braid and let it roll down my back behind me. Perching on a camp stool, I shut my eyes and sat in silence as Oria patiently fingered the long braid apart and then brushed it out until it lay in a shining cloak down nearly to my knees. The steady brushing was soothing, and I felt all the tensions of the long day drain out of me.

When she was done, I said, "Thanks, Ria. That's as good as an afternoon nap in the summer."

"A shame you have to put it up again," she said, smiling. "It's so pretty—the color of autumn leaves. Promise you'll never cut it."

"I won't. It's the only thing I have left to share with my mother, the color of our hair. And she always wanted me to grow it out." My fingers worked quickly from old habit as I braided it up again, wrapped it twice around my head, and tucked the end in. "But I can't parade around in long hair during a war. Or, I suppose I could, except then I'd end up carrying half the mountain in it."

"You can wear it down after we win, then, and start a new fashion."

"You'll be the one starting the fashions," I said, laughing up at her.

"Duchess Oria," she said, swishing around my tiny tent. "New silk shoes every day—twice a day! I can hardly wait."

"That'll do," Julen said to Oria. She was vigorously brushing mud off my alternate pair of woolen trousers. "You stop your non-

38

sense and go and get your rest. We'll have to make a supply run again tomorrow." Oria stuck her tongue out at her mother, grinned at me, and ran out. Julen laid my other tunic down. "This is the best I can make of these trousers; the mud will not come out. Your brother's old tunic looks even worse," she said, frowning heavily. "I wish I could wash these properly! Even so, they wouldn't look much better. 'Tis shameful, you not dressing to befit your station. Especially on this day."

I dropped onto my bedroll, grinning. "For whom?" I asked. "Everyone has seen me like this since I was small. And truth to tell, Oria would look a lot prettier in fancy clothes than I would."

Julen's square, worn face looked formidable as she considered this. She said slowly, " 'Tisn't proper. When I grew up, we dressed to fit our places in life. Then you knew who was what at a glance —and how to deal with 'em."

"But that means an orderly life, and when has Tlanth been orderly?" I asked, sobering. "Not in my memory."

Julen gave a short nod. "It's just not right, your runnin' bare-foot and ignorant with the village brats. I count my two among 'em," she added with a wry smile.

"But they're my friends," I said, leaning on one elbow. "We know each other. We'll defend each other to the death. You think Faeruk and the rest would have left their patches of farm or their work to follow us if I'd stayed in the castle, spending tax money on gowns and putting on airs?"

Julen pursed her lips. "Friends in war—and I hope you'll re-member us when things are put right. But you know we all will eventually have to take up our work again, and you won't be know-ing how to have friends among your own kind."

"I don't miss what I never had."

"I've said my piece. Except," Julen added strongly, "I'll con-tinue to curse the day Galdran Merindar's mother didn't strangle him at birth."

"Now, *that*," I said with a laugh, "is a fine idea, and one I'll join with enthusiasm! Now, tell me this: What's amiss with Hrani? Both her older children are fine. I saw them in camp tonight, joking around with the others. Yet she looked unhappy."

Julen's lips compressed. "It's the youngest. Tuel came down with messages from the hideaway today, bringing some of yon blooms." Julen lowered her voice. "Hrani's baby is fine, it's just that she's no longer a baby, and Hrani wasn't there to see her leave off diapers and use the Waste Spell." She gave a quick look over her shoulder to see if any men happened to have sneaked into the tent and were listening.

I nodded. "So they had the ceremony, and Hrani was here with us instead of welcoming her daughter to childhood. Now I see. Poor Hrani!"

"Don't say aught of it to her. Might make her feel worse." Julen sighed and pointed at my other tunic. "Change now, before you catch your death."

"All right," I said, feigning a yawn. It wouldn't do for her to figure out what I was up to. "And then I think I'll get some sleep."

She bustled about the tent a little while longer while I hastily changed. I wrapped myself up in my blankets and lay down on the cot. By the time she was done I was almost warm. She blew out the candle and left.

Moonlight flooded my tent when I rose, jammed my feet into my winter mocs, pulled on my ancient hat, and slipped out. The ground was still muddy, but I had long ago learned how to move across soggy ground. The air was now still and almost balmy. As I slipped between the tents, tugging my battered hat close about my ears, I looked up, awed by the spectacular blaze of stars scattered gleaming across the sky. Both moons were up, still slivers, but their silvery glow gave me just enough light to make out my pathway.

A few paces beyond the last tent, I heard a sudden noise and a voice: "Who's there?"

Pleased at this evidence of an alert sentry, I said, "It's Meliara, Devan. I'm going scouting."

"Countess!" Devan dropped down from a tree branch into my path and squinted into my face. "Alone?"

"I think I'll be the faster this way," I said. "And it's so beautiful tonight, I think I'll enjoy the going."

He paused, a big man used to millstones and bushels of wheat, not to clutching a sword. "Ain't there someone else to go?"

"This is *my* mission," I said.

"Well, be safe," he said, hoisting himself back up into the mighty tree. "And quick. I'll be on the watch for your return."

I thanked him and sped down the pathway, stopping only to check my bearings. Well as I knew the terrain, everything is different at night—unless night is what one is accustomed to. Picturing my map, I located myself in reference to our camp, and to where theirs was likeliest to be.

What I had to watch out for was their sentries, who, since the camp couldn't possibly be hidden, probably would be. Debegri had kept them close, probably to guard his precious person the better, but the Marquis sent his out at much wider range—something we'd discovered too late, which had precipitated our first, and worst, battle.

Deciding to approach from above and on the other side of the river, I made my way swiftly along an old animal path to where I knew there was a big tree bridging the ravine. Careful scanning revealed no humans about, so I crossed the massive trunk without looking down. Not far away was a jut of rock from which a good portion of the valley below could be seen. I lay behind some shrubs and watched the rock's silhouette for a time. There was nothing obviously amiss, but as the approach was bare, affording a clear field of vision, I didn't want to risk walking until I knew it was safe.

Three times I'd almost decided to move, then changed my mind and watched a bit longer before I saw what I'd feared: One of the unevennesses on the jut stirred. Just slightly—but it was enough to make it plain that one soldier, and probably more, crouched there in the rubble.

So I had to find another way down, but at least—I told myself as I carefully withdrew back into the shrubbery—I'd been right about the location of their camp.

With painstaking care I made my way to another slope and climbed one of the great sky-sweeping pines. Peering down through a gap in the branches, I saw the camp at last. And what I saw made my heart thud with dismay. The entire hillside below gleamed with little reddish campfires, not just dozens of them, but nearer a dozen dozen. Where indeed had they gotten so many Fire Sticks? I knew they couldn't be burning wood, for then there would have been smoke, and smell, and possibly the drums of the Hill Folk. How could Galdran justify forcing his soldiers to take Sticks from so many families?

Anyway, I sat and tried to estimate how many Fire Sticks they had, and therefore how many unknown households must be going cold. Then I tried to estimate the rows of tents that I could just make out between the fires.

Had Galdran sent his *entire* army up against us?

I clutched the swaying branch, pine scent sharp in my nostrils, and stared down, realizing slowly what this meant. There was no way we could win. Even with the old commander against us, the sheer weight of numbers would have ground us down to nothing. But under this new commander, how long would it take before Galdran had Bran and me paraded down the Street of the Sun on our way to a public execution?

And what about our people?

And after they were disposed of, what about the Covenant?

I closed my fists and pounded lightly on the tree branch. We had to do something—fast! But what?

All I could think as I climbed down was that desperate situations required desperate measures. And then I had to laugh at myself as I ran up the path. That sounded properly heroic, but how to make it *work*?

I looked up at the black interlacing of leaves, through which the rainbow-hued stars made a pattern of heedless beauty. The stars, the mountains, the rustling trees formed a silent testimony to the shortsighted futility of the humans who struggled below. I thought of Hrani missing her child's passing from the innocent abandon of babyhood into childhood. And suddenly I wished I were shed of the war, shed of hunger, of tiredness, and dirt, and could wander at will through the forest, enjoying its peace.

Only, one cannot put aside a war, even for a moment.

Ah, Branaric.

My head was back, my eyes still on the stars as I walked. All the warning I had was a metallic *klingg!* and then red-hot pain blazed from my ankle up to my skull and closed my consciousness for an immeasurable time behind a fiery red wall.

The first thought to penetrate was a desperate one: *Don't scream, don't scream.* My breath rasped in my throat as I struggled up. My nose stung, and I sneezed—I had landed facedown on a sprig of stingflower.

I ran my fingers lightly over the fanged steel closed around my ankle, whimpering, "Got to get it off, got to get it off..."

Why had I refused to touch them, to learn how to disable them? And how came this one here? As another white-hot spear of agony shot through me, I fell back, realized that this one had not been on the map. My hand fumbled for the sprig of stingflower and I sniffed at it, sneezing again. The pain was terrific, but this was better than fainting. *The herb is fresh,* I thought, glad I could still think. *Keep busy... think... They must have laid this one just a while ago, and there's been no time yet to write it down...*

I rolled to my knees, wondering if I could somehow manage to walk despite the thing, but just the slightest movement flattened me again. Then I heard crashing in the shrubbery down the trail, and when I turned my head, the weird fractured shadows cast by bobbing torches hurt my eyes.

Our people wouldn't be carrying torches so close to their *camp—*

The thought wormed its way through my fading consciousness.

I had just enough presence of mind to fling myself back into the sheltering branches of a spreading fern before the roaring in my ears overwhelmed me and cast me into darkness.

A strong taste tingled in my mouth and burned its way into my throat. I gasped when the banked fire of pain sent flame licking up my body.

"Another sip."

Something pressed insistently against my lips, which parted. Another wash of pungent fluid cleared some of the haze from my brain. I swallowed, gasped again. My eyes teared, opened, and I drew a long, shaky breath.

"That's it," the same voice said with satisfaction. "Here y'are, m'lord. She's awake."

"Bran?" I croaked.

"What was that?" a new voice murmured, on my other side.

"Your trap," I said, my voice hardly strong enough to be called a whisper. I tried to blink my eyes into focus, but my vision stayed hazy. "I knew . . . this would happen . . . to one of us."

"Fair enough," the new voice said, amusement shading the slow, drawling words. "It's happened to nine of us."

A harsh laugh from a different direction smote my ears. "Take this fool out and hang her," this new voice grated. "And the trap with her. Let the slinking rebels find *that*."

"Softly, Baron, softly," said the quiet voice.

The voices—all unfamiliar—the words penetrated then, and I realized I was in the hands of the enemy.

SIX

THE HAZE PROMPTLY SWALLOWED ME, AND IT WAS A long time before I woke up again. This time I was aware of a headache first, and of correspondingly intense pain radiating up my left leg. Even though I couldn't lift my head I could move it; within the space of two breaths I realized I was lying in a tent, and there was a young woman wearing a brown cloak with the sigil of a healer stitched on one side.

My gaze traveled up to her face. She was young, with ordinary features and patient brown eyes. Her dark hair was drawn back into a single braid clipped short at shoulder length.

"Here's water," she said. "Drink."

With practiced care she lifted my head, and I slurped eagerly at the water. My lips were dry; my mouth felt worse. When she offered a second dipperful, I accepted gratefully.

"Think you some soup would go down well?" she asked, her voice neutral.

"Try." My voice sounded like an old frog's.

She nodded and left the tent. I heard the murmur of voices, and then I remembered, with a pang of anger-laced fear, that I was a prisoner. As if to corroborate it, my fingers moved to my waist, found that my knife belt was indeed gone.

Wincing against the headache, I rose on my elbows, looked down at my legs. The one was securely wrapped in a bandage. My moc was gone. I wiggled my bare toes experimentally, and then wished I hadn't.

The tent flap opened a moment later, and the healer reappeared with a steaming mug in either hand. The familiar smell of camp soup met my nose, and the light, summer-fields aroma of lister-blossom tea.

She offered the tea first. Knowing it would help ease the pain a little, I drank it down, wincing as it scalded my tongue and throat. Even so, it was wonderful. The soup was next, and way in the back of my mind a bubble of humor arose at how much it tasted just like the stuff we'd been eating in our camp these long weeks. Only, this had a few more spices to render the boiled vegetables a little more palatable.

When I was done I lay back, exhausted by even that much effort. "Thanks," I said. Again the healer nodded, then she went out.

I closed my eyes, feeling sleep steal over me; but the pleasant lassitude fled when the tent flap opened again, this time pulled by a rough hand. Cold air swirled in. I blinked up at a burly helmeted soldier. He held the tent flap aside for a much lighter-boned man, who walked in wearing an anonymous black cloak. The guard let the flap fall, and I heard the gravel crunch under his boots as he took up position outside the tent.

The new arrival sank down onto the camp stool the healer had used, but he didn't say anything, so for a short time we studied one another's faces in the dim light. Large gray eyes surveyed me from my filthy scalp to my bandaged leg. I could read nothing in the man's face beyond that leisurely assessment, so I just stared back, trying to gather my wits as I catalogued his features: a straight nose, the chiseled bones of someone at least Bran's age, a long mouth with the deep corners of someone on the verge of a laugh. All this framed by long pale blond hair tied simply back, under a broad-brimmed but undecorated black hat. His rank was impossible to guess, but his job wasn't—he had to be an interrogator.

So I braced myself for interrogation.

And watched his eyes register this fact, and those mouth corners deepen for just a moment. Then his face blanked again, his gaze resting on mine with mild interest as he said, "What is your name?"

It took a moment for the words to register—for me to realize he did not know who I was! His eyes narrowed; he had seen my reaction, then—and I stirred, which effectively turned my surprise into a wince of pain.

"Name?" he said again. His voice was vaguely familiar, but the vagueness remained when I tried to identify it.

"I am very much afraid," he said presently, "that your probable future is not the kind to excite general envy, but I promise I can make it much easier if you cooperate."

"Eat mud," I croaked.

He smiled slightly, both mouth and eyes. The reaction of angerless humor was unexpected, but before I could try to assess it, he said, "You'll have to permit me to be more explicit. If you do not willingly discourse with me, I expect the King will send some of his experts, who will exert themselves to get the information we require, with your cooperation or without it." He leaned one hand across his knee, watching still with that air of mild interest—as if he had all the time in the world. His hand was long fingered, slim in form; he might have been taken for some minor Court scribe except for the callused palm of one who has trained all his life with the sword.

The import of his words hit me then, and with them came more fear—and more anger. "What is it you want to know?" I asked.

His eyes narrowed slightly. "Where the Astiars' camp lies, and their immediate plans, will do for a start."

"Their camp lies in their land...on which you are the trespasser...and their plans are to...rid the kingdom of...a

47

rotten tyrant." It took effort to get that out. But I was reasonably proud of my nasty tone.

His brows lifted. They were long and winged, which contributed to that air of faint question. "Well," he said, laying his hands flat on his knees for a moment, then he swung to his feet with leisurely grace. "We have a fire-eater on our hands, I see. But then one doesn't expect to find abject cowardice in spies." He stepped toward the flap, then paused and said over his shoulder, "You should probably rest while you can. I fear you have an unpleasant set of interviews ahead of you."

With that he lifted the flap and went out.

Leaving me to some very bleak thoughts.

He did that on purpose, I told myself after a long interval during which I tried not to imagine what those "experts" would try first in order to get me to blab—and how long I'd last. I'd faced the prospect of dying in battle and was ready enough, but I'd never considered the idea of torture.

And the worst of it is, I thought dismally, *there's nothing to be gained, really. We don't have any kind of master plan, and the camp will probably be changed by tomorrow. But if I say any of that willingly, then I am a coward, and they'll be sure to let everyone know it soon's they find out who I am.*

As soon as—

Think! My head ached anew, but I forced myself to follow the thought to its logical conclusion. The enemy did not know who I was. *Which means they cannot use me against Bran.*

That was the secret I had to keep my teeth closed on as long as I could, I realized. My person was worth more than what was in my head—*if* Galdran found out.

So he can't find out, I resolved, and I lay back flat, closed my eyes, and tried my best to suspend my thoughts so I could sleep.

When I woke again, I was in darkness.

Fighting my way to awareness, I realized I'd heard sharp voices.

Yells echoed back and forth, calling commands to different ridings; from the distance there came the clang and clash of steel.

It's Bran, I thought, elated and fearful. *He's attacking the camp!*

As if in answer, I heard his voice. "Mel! *Mel!*"

I rolled to my knees, fighting against invisible knives of pain. One more cry of "Mel!" at slightly more of a distance enabled me to gather my courage and stand up.

Diving through the tent flap, I screamed with all my failing strength, *"BRAN!"* And I clutched at the tent to keep myself from falling full-length on the muddy ground. A light mist bathed my face, making me shiver—a distant part of me acknowledged that in addition to everything else I had a pretty hot fever going.

"Meliara! Mel! *Mel!*" A number of voices took up the cry, and I realized that all our people must have attacked.

Again I gathered all my strength and started forward. Which was a mistake. My left foot simply refused to carry my weight.

I started to fall, felt hard hands catching one of my arms. My leg jolted—and thank goodness, that finished me.

When I woke again there were voices, only this time close, and they hurt my ears. A particularly harsh one prevailed. As I struggled against waves of fog to identify that voice, some of its words came clear: "...your responsibility, unless you want to formally relinquish her to me. I know what to do with rebels..."

The fog closed in again, clearing to a steady roaring noise that slowly resolved into the sound of rain on the tent roof. Again there were voices in the distance, but the lassitude of heavy fever made it impossible for me to make sense of what I heard.

The next thing I was aware of was the fitful red beating of fire through my eyelids. Someone lifted my head and pressed a cup to my lips. I smelled listerblossom tea, with another, sharper scent beneath it. I opened my eyes and drank. The taste was bitter, but I was thirsty.

The bitterness had to be some kind of sleep herb; my head

seemed to separate from my body as I was jostled and moved about. But the pain stayed at a distance, for which I was grateful, and I gave up trying to fight for consciousness.

When I did come to again, it was to the slow recognition of patterned movement. Next I realized that I was more or less upright, kept in place by the uncompromising grip of an arm. And at last I saw that I was on horseback and someone was with me.

"Bran?" I murmured hopefully.

The arm did not slacken its grip as its owner hesitated, then said, "It desolates me to disappoint you, but your brother is not here. Despite two really praiseworthy attempts at rescue." I recognized that drawling voice: the interrogator's.

The hint of amusement irritated me, and sick and hurt as I was, I simply had to retort *some*thing. "Glad . . . at least . . . you're desolated."

As a crack it was pretty weak, but the amusement deepened in the light voice above my ear as he added, "I must add, when your hill rebels get truly riled, they do fight well. We didn't catch any of 'em. Several dead, but they're of no use to anyone. And they accounted for rather more of us than they ought to have."

"*Haha*," I gloated.

The voice continued, polite but utterly devoid of any emotion save that hint of amusement: "Your hat disappeared somewhere the other night, and it did not seem appropriate under the circumstances to request someone in our army to surrender a replacement."

"It's of no consequence—" I began loftily, then I grunted with pain as the horse made a misstep and veered around some obstruction in the road.

And a new fact registered: *He knows who I am.*

Which means we must be on the way to Remalna-city—and Galdran.

A sick feeling of terror seized my insides, and I was glad the man holding me could not see my face. My head was tucked against his shoulder, with my left leg as straight as possible across the horse's withers, my right dangling. I thought immediately of struggling, trying to fight free, except I remembered what had happened when I had tried to take a step.

Well, then, somehow I have to escape—and take the horse, I told myself. *There's almost a three-day journey ahead. Anything can happen if I am on the watch.*

I turned my attention to my surroundings. We were riding at a slow, steady pace downhill toward the east. The long bands of clouds above were cold blue on top, their undersides yellow and pink, and the reflected peachy gold glow touched the valleys and fields with warm light. Behind me, I knew, were the high mountains and ancient, tangled forest where I'd grown up. Below me the mountains opened slowly into farmland, with dark marches of forest reaching toward the distant sea. Such profligate beauty lifted my spirits, and despite the situation, I couldn't believe I would come to ill.

Unfortunately, this elevated mood disappeared with the sun. For the light steadily grew more diffuse and lost its warmth, the shadows closed in, and a steady, drizzling rain began to fall. Faintly, in the distance, I heard bells tolling for blue-change, and even they sounded mournful. My various aches seemed to increase with the darkness, and once or twice when the tired horse stumbled, wrenching my left leg, I couldn't help making noise, but I turned each into a muttered curse.

My captor left the road before it was completely dark, and rode with a sense of sureness that indicated he knew the terrain. After a time we stopped in a secluded glade against a rocky palisade, under the sheltering branches of a great-grandfather oak. A short distance away a little stream plashed off the rocks and wound its way among the trees. The east wind did not penetrate there, nor did much of the rain.

In silence the man reined in his horse, dismounted, lifted me down to a high grassy spot that was scarcely damp. In the gathering gloom he tended to his horse, which presently cropped at the grass. My eyes had become accustomed to the darkness; the flare of light from a Fire Stick, and the reddish flicker of a fire, startled me.

At first I turned away, for the unsteady flame hurt my eyes, but after a time the prospect of warmth brought me around, and I started inching toward the fire.

The man looked up, dropped what he was doing, and took a step toward me. "I can carry you," he said.

I waved him off. "I'll do it myself," I said shortly, thinking, *Why be polite now? So I'll be in a good mood when you dump me in Galdran's dungeon?*

He hesitated. I ignored him and turned my attention to easing forward. After a moment he returned to whatever he had been doing. After a little experimenting, I found that it was easiest to sit backward and inchworm along, dragging my left leg.

Soon enough I was near to his fire, which was properly built in a ring of rocks. Using the tip of his rapier, he held out chunks of bread with cheese, toasting them just enough. The smell made my mouth water.

In silence he divided the food into two portions, laying mine on a flat rock near my hand.

Then he held up a camp kettle. "Want tea? Or just water?"

"Tea," I said.

He walked off toward the waterfall. I peered after him into the gloom, saw the horse standing near the pool where the water fell. One chance of escape gone. I'd never get to the horse before he could stop me.

With a small sense of relief, I turned my attention to the bread. I was suddenly ravenous, and even though the cheese was still hot, I wolfed my share down and licked my fingers to catch the last crumbs.

By then the man had returned and set the kettle among the

embers. Then he looked up, paused, then picked up his share of the bread and reached over to put it in front of me.

"That's yours," I said.

"You appear to need it more than I do," he said, looking amused. "Go ahead. I won't starve."

I picked up the bread, feeling a weird sense of unreality: Did he expect me to be grateful? The situation was so strange I simply had to turn it into absurdity—it was either that or sink into fear and apprehension. "Well, does it matter if I starve?" I said. "Or do Galdran's torturers require only plump victims for their arts?"

The man had started to unload something from the saddlebag at his side, but he stopped and looked up with that contemplative gaze again, his broad-brimmed black hat just shadowing his eyes. "The situation has altered," he said slowly. "You must perceive how your value has changed."

His words, his tone—as if he expected an outbreak of hysterics—fired my indignation. Maybe my situation was desperate, and sooner than later I was going to be having nightmares about it—but not for the entertainment of some drawling Court-bred flunky.

"He'll try to use me against my brother," I said in my flattest voice.

"I rather suspect he will be successful. In the space of one day your brother and his adherents attacked our camp twice. It would appear they are not indifferent to your fate."

I remembered then that he had said something about an attack earlier, but I'd scarcely comprehended what he meant. "Do you know who was killed?" I asked quickly.

The firelight played over his face. He watched me with a kind of narrow-eyed assessment impossible to interpret. "You know them all, don't you," he commented.

"Of course I do," I said. "You don't know who—or you just won't tell me, for some rock-headed reason?"

He smiled. "Your determined bravado is a refreshment to the

spirit. But if you know them all by name, then the loss of each is immeasurably greater. Why did you do it? Did you really think you could take a few hundred ill-trained village people into war and expect anything but defeat?"

I opened my mouth to retort, then realized I'd be spoiling what little strategy we did have.

But then he said wryly, "Or did you expect the rest of the kingdom to follow your heroic example and rise up against the King?"

Which is, of course, exactly what we *had* expected.

"So they sit like overfed fowl and watch Galdran Merindar break the Covenant by making secret pacts to sell our woods over-seas?" I retorted.

He paused in the act of reaching for the camp jug. "Break the Covenant? How do you know about that? I don't recall you've ever been to Court."

Tell him about Azmus, and the intercepted letter, and have him send minions to make certain both disappeared? No chance. "I just know. That's all *you* need to know. But even if it weren't true, Debegri would still go up to take the County of Tlanth by force. Can't any of you Court people see that if it happens to us, it can happen to you? Or are you too stupid?"

"Possibly," he said, still with that dispassionate amusement. "It's also possible your . . . somewhat misguided actions are inspired by misguided sources, shall we say?"

"Say what you want," I retorted. "It's not like I can duff off in a huff if you're impolite."

He laughed softly, then shook his head. "I ought not to bait you. I apologize."

The implication seemed pretty clear: Soon enough I'd have a hard time of it. The prospect silenced me.

He didn't seem to notice as he brought out the jug and then poured two mugs of steaming water. A moment later he opened a little bag and brought out dried leaves, which he cast into one mug.

Another bag provided leaves for the other mug. The wonderful scent of tea wafted through the air. I did not recognize the blend —or blends. Instinct made me sigh; then I realized I'd done it and wished I hadn't.

The man came around, set a cup down by my hand. "Are you very uncomfortable?"

"Does it matter?" I said, and wrapped my chilled hands around the cup—which was not of the battered metal I'd expected, but very fine ceramic. Exquisite gilding ran round the lip, a stylized braid of argan leaves.

"Whether it does or not, you shall have a better conveyance on the morrow," he said. "Drink your tea and sleep. We shall continue our discourse when you have had some rest."

I couldn't resist one more crack. "Is that a promise or a threat?"

He just smiled.

SEVEN

MY FIRST DUTY WAS TO ESCAPE. AS I LAY UNDER THE blanket the man had given me, I tried to figure out how I might get myself to where the horse stood without rousing its owner from his slumbers. Once I was on the animal's back, it wouldn't matter if the man woke up—in fact, it might be nice to see that Court-bred composure shattered.

I drifted off while estimating steps from tree to shrub, and didn't waken until the thud of horses' hooves under my ear brought me to drowsy wakefulness.

Waves of exhaustion ebbed and flowed over me as I watched in dreamy bemusement. The interrogator still sat in the same place, staring down into some kind of stone that cast a weird bluish light over his face and glowed in two bright pinpoints in his eyes. It was magic. A summons-stone. A rarity that made me wonder just who he was—or whether we had vastly underestimated Galdran's access to wizard wares. Beyond him the soft, steady *plop-plop* of raindrops on leaves tapped out a pleasant rhythm.

I think I drifted again, without meaning to, because when I opened my eyes again it was to see a young equerry dismount from a hard-breathing charger and bow low. "My lord," she said, holding out another blue-glowing stone.

The man sat where he was, merely taking the stone as he said, "Your report."

"Baron Debegri has dispatched your orders about the carriage. It should be waiting at the Lumm-at-Akaeriki bridge by green-change tomorrow."

"And our friends the Tlanthi?"

"Are silent, my lord. Your message was sent under white flag, and Lord Jastra reported it was given into their hands. Nothing from that time until I left."

"Promising," was the answer. "It seems likely we'll be back in civilization well in advance of the Spring Festival, after all," he finished, the Court drawl very pronounced. "Return. Tell the Baron to be so good as to carry on as ordered."

The equerry bowed again. I saw her stifle a yawn as she threw herself into the saddle; she was soon out of the circle of firelight, but I listened to the sound of the horse's hooves diminish, questions looming in my mind. As I struggled with them, I sank once more under the tide of slumber and didn't waken until the lovely scent of tea worked its way into my dreams and banished them.

I sat up, fought against dizziness. Somewhere in the distance a single bell rang out the pattern for gold-candles and the beginning of another day.

"Drink."

The cup was near to hand. I rose on one elbow and reached for it. Some sips later I felt immeasurably better. My eyesight cleared, and so did my thoughts.

I remembered the interlude during the night, and frowned across the fire at my companion. He looked exactly the same as ever—as if he'd sat up for a single time measure and not for an entire night. The plain hat, simply tied hair, ordinary clothing un-marked by any device; I squinted, trying to equate this slight figure with that arrogant plume-helmed commander riding on the ridge above the last battle. *But if he is who I think he is, they're used to being up all night at their stupid Court parties*, I thought grimly.

"You seem to know who I am," I said. "Who are you?"

"Does it matter?"

His use of my own words the night before surprised me a little. Did he expect flattery? Supposedly those so-refined Court aristocrats lived on it as anyone else lives on bread and drink. I considered my answer, wanting to make certain it was not even remotely complimentary. "I'm exactly as unlikely to blab our secrets to an anonymous flunky as I am to a Court decoration with a reputation as a gambler and a fop," I said finally.

" 'Court decoration'?" he repeated, with a faint smile. The strengthening light of dawn revealed telltale marks under his eyes. So he *was* tired. I was obscurely glad.

"Yes," I said, pleased to expand on my insult. "My father's term."

"You've never wished to meet a...Court decoration for yourself?"

"No." Then I added cheerily, "Well, maybe when I was a child."

The Marquis of Shevraeth, Galdran's commander-in-chief, grinned. It was the first real grin I'd seen on his face, as if he were struggling to hold in laughter. Setting his cup down, he made a graceful half-bow from his seat on the other side of the fire and said, "Delighted to make your acquaintance, Lady Meliara."

I sniffed.

"And now that I've been thoroughly put in my place," he said, "let us leave my way of life and proceed to yours. I take it your revolt is not engineered for the benefit of your fellow-nobles, or as an attempt to reestablish your mother's blood claim through the Calahanras family. Wherefore is it, then?"

I looked up in surprise. "There ought to be no mystery obscuring our reasons. Did you not trouble to read the letter we sent to Galdran Merindar before he sent Debegri against us? It was addressed to the entire Court, and our reasons were stated as plainly as we could write them—and all our names signed to it."

"Assume that the letter was somehow suppressed," he said dryly. "Can you summarize its message?"

"Easy," I said promptly. "We went to war on behalf of the Hill Folk, whose Covenant Galdran wants to break. But not just for them. We also want to better the lives of the people of Remalna: the ordinary folk who've been taxed into poverty, or driven from their farms, or sent into hastily constructed mines, all for Galdran's personal glory. And I guess for the rest of yours as well, for whose money are you spending on those fabulous Court clothes you never wear twice? Your father still holds the Renselaeus principality—or has he ceded it to Galdran at last? Isn't it, too, taxed and farmed to the bone so that you can outshine all the rest of those fools at Court?"

All the humor had gone out of his face, leaving it impossible to read. He said, "Since the kind of rumor about Court life that you seem to regard as truth also depicts us as inveterate liars, I will not waste time attempting to defend or deny. Let us instead discuss your eventual goal. Supposing," he said, reaching to pour more tea into my cup—as if we were in a drawing room, and not sitting outside in the chill dawn, in grimy clothes, on either side of a fire just as we were on either side of a war—"Supposing you were to defeat the King. What then? Kill all the nobles in Athanarel and set yourselves up as rustic King and Queen?"

I remembered father's whisper as he lay dying: *You can take Remalna, and you will be better rulers than any Merindar ever was.*

It had sounded fine then, but the thought of giving any hint of that to this blank-faced Court idler made me uncomfortable. I shook my head. "We didn't want to kill anyone. Not even Galdran, until he sent Debegri to break the Covenant and take our lands. As for ruling, yes we would, if no one else better came along. We were doing it not for ourselves but for the kingdom. Disbelieve it all you want, but there's the truth of it."

"Finish your tea," he said. "Before we find our way to a more comfortable conveyance, I am very much afraid we're both in for a distasteful interlude." He reached into the saddlebag and pulled out a wad of bandage ticking and some green leaves.

I sat up suddenly, winced, then stretched my hands over the bandage on my ankle, which (I dared a quick look) was filthy. "Oh no, you don't."

"I promised Mistress Kylar. And if I don't keep that promise, chances are you might lose that foot. So brace up. I'll be as quick as I can."

"Give me the stuff and let me do it," I said. "I know how. I've helped patch up all our wounded."

"Here's a knife. Let's see how far you get in taking the old bandage off." And he tossed a dagger across the fire. It spun through the air and landed hilt-deep in the ground next to my hand.

"Lucky throw," I said snidely, suspecting that it hadn't been. He said nothing, which confirmed my suspicions. So I turned my back in order to avoid seeing that bland gray gaze, and I yanked the knife free. At first I wanted to wipe it clean on my clothes, but a quick perusal of my person reminded me that I'd already been wearing grimy clothes before I'd walked into the trap, fallen full length in the mud, and spent two days lying in a tent. So I wiped the dagger on the grass, then slit the bindings on the bandage. Spots of brown that had leaked through and hardened on the outside of the bandage warned me that this was probably going to be the least favorite of all my life experiences so far.

I gulped, held my breath, pulled the bandage quickly away. The keem leaves were all wrinkled and old. I started to pull the first one free, gasped, and was nearly overwhelmed by a sudden loud rushing in my ears.

When it subsided, my companion was right next to me. The dagger was back in its sheath at his belt, and he handed me a length of wood that had fallen from a nearby tree. "Hang on," he said briskly. "I'll be as fast as I can."

I barely had time to take hold of the wood with both hands; then I felt warm water pour over my ankle. I didn't squeak, or cry, or make any sound—but as soon as the fresh keem leaves were on my torn flesh and the new bandage was being wrapped quickly around and around, I clutched that wood tight and started cursing, not pausing except to draw breath.

When it was done and he took the mess away to bury, I lay back and breathed deeply, doing my best to settle my boiling stomach.

"All right," he said, "that's that. Now it's time to go, if we're to reach Lumm by green-change." He whistled, and the dapple-gray trotted obediently up, head tossing.

I realized I ought to have been more observant about chances for escape, and I wondered if there were any chance of taking him by surprise now.

First to see if I could even stand. As he went about the chore of resaddling the horse, I eased myself to my feet. I took my time at it, too, not just because my ankle was still protesting its recent rebandaging; I wanted to seem as decrepit as possible. My head felt weirdly light when I made it to my feet, and I had to hang on to a branch of the oak—my foot simply wouldn't take any weight. As soon as I tried it, my middle turned to water and I groped for the branch again.

Which meant if I did try anything, it was going to have to be within reach of the horse. I watched for a moment as he lashed down the saddlebags then rammed the rapier into the saddle sheath. There was already that knife at his belt. This did not look promising, I thought, remembering all the lessons on close fighting that Khesot had drilled into us. *If your opponent is better armed and has the longer reach, then surprise is your only ally. And then you'd better hope he's half-asleep.* Well, the fellow had to be tired if he'd sat up all night, I thought, looking around for any kind of weapon.

The branch he'd handed me to hang on to was still lying at my feet. I stooped—cautiously—and snatched it up. Dropping one end, I discovered that it made a serviceable cane, and with its aid I hobbled my way a few paces, watching carefully for any rocks or roots that might trip me.

Then a step in the grass made me look up. The Marquis was

right in front of me, and he was a lot taller than he looked seated across a campfire. In one hand were the horse's reins, and he held the other hand out in an offer to boost me up. I noticed again that his palm was crossed with calluses, indicating years of swordwork. I grimaced, reluctantly surrendering my image of the Court-bred fop who never lifted anything heavier than a fork.

"Ready?" His voice was the same as always—or almost the same.

I tipped my head back to look at his face, instantly suspicious. Despite his compressed lips he was clearly on the verge of laughter.

For a moment I longed, with all my heart, to swing my stick right at his head. My fingers gripped . . . and his palm turned, just slightly; but I knew a block readying when I saw one. The strong possibility that anything I attempted would lead directly to an ignominious defeat did not improve my mood at all, but I dropped the stick and wiped my hand down the side of my rumpled tunic.

Vowing I'd see that smile wiped off his cursed face, I said shortly, "Let's get it over with."

He put his hands on my waist and boosted me up onto the horse—and I couldn't help but notice it didn't take all that much effort.

All right, defeat so far, I thought as I winced and gritted my way through arranging my leg much as it had been on the previous ride. *All I have to do is catch him in a single unwary moment* . . . He mounted behind me and we started off, while I indulged myself with the image of grabbing that stick and conking him right across his smiling face.

The less said about that morning's ride, the better. I would have been uncomfortable even if I'd been riding with Branaric, for my leg ached steadily from the jarring of the horse's pace. To be riding along in the clasp of an enemy just made my spirits feel the worse.

We only had one conversation, right at the start, when he apologized for the discomfort of the ride and reminded me that there would be a carriage—and reasonable comfort—before the day was gone.

I said, in as surly a tone as possible, "You might have thought of that before we left. I mean, since no one asked my opinion on the matter."

"It was purely an impulse of disinterested benevolence that precipitated our departure," he responded equably—as if I'd been as polite as one of his simpering Court ladies.

"What do you mean by that?"

"I mean that it seemed very likely that your brother and his adherents were going to mount another rescue attempt, and this time there was no chance of our being taken by surprise."

He paused, letting me figure that out. He meant the King's warriors would have killed everyone, or else taken them all prisoner, and he had forestalled such a thing. Why he should want to prevent this opportunity to defeat all our people at once didn't make sense to me; I kept quiet.

He went on after a moment, "Since the King requires a report on our progress, and as it seemed expedient to remove you, I decided to combine the two. It appears to have worked, at least for a time."

Which meant he'd stalled Branaric—with what? Threats against my life if our people tried anything? The thought made me wild with anger, with a determination to escape so strong that for a time it took all my self-control not to fling myself from that horse and run, bad leg or no.

For at last I faced the real truth: that by my own carelessness, I might very well have graveled our entire cause. I knew my brother. Branaric would not risk my life—and this man seemed to have figured that much out.

The Marquis made a couple other attempts at conversation, but I ignored him. I have to confess that, for a short time, hot tears of rage and self-loathing stung my eyes and dripped down my face. I didn't trust my voice; the only consolation I had for my eroding self-respect was that my face couldn't be seen.

When the tears had dried at last, and I had taken a surreptitious swipe at my nose and eyes with my sleeve, I gritted my teeth and turned my thoughts back to escape.

EIGHT

THE SUN WAS DIRECTLY OVERHEAD AND MERCI-
lessly hot when we reached the Akaeriki River. What ought to have
been a cool early-spring day—as it probably was, high in our
mountains—felt like the middle of summer, and my entire body
protested by turning into one giant itch. Even my braid, gritty and
damp, felt repellent.

In addition to everything else, not long after the village bells
all over the valley merrily rang the changeover from gold to green,
my stomach started rumbling with hunger.

It was a relief when we reached the village of Lumm. We did
not go into it but rode on the outskirts. When the great mage-built
bridge came into view I felt Shevraeth's arm tighten as he looked
this way and that.

On a grassy sward directly opposite the approach to the bridge
a plain carriage waited with no markings on its sides, the wheels
and lower portions muddy. The only sign that this might not be
some inn's rental equipment were the five high-bred horses waiting
nearby, long lines attached to their bits. A boy wearing the garb of
a stable hand sat on a large rock holding the horses' lines; nearby
a footman and a driver, both in unmarked clothing but wearing
servants' hats, stood conversing in between sips from hip flagons.

Steady traffic, mostly merchants, passed by, but no one gave them more than a cursory glance.

The gray threaded through a caravan of laden carts. As soon as the waiting servants saw us, the flagons were hastily stowed, the horse boy leaped to his feet, and all three bowed low.

"Hitch them up," said the Marquis.

The boy sprang to the horses' mouths and the driver to the waiting harnesses as the footman moved to the stirrup of the gray.

No one spoke. With a minimum of fuss the Marquis dismounted, pulled me down himself, and deposited me in the carriage on a seat strewn with pillows. Then he shut the door and walked away.

By then the driver was on her box, and the horse boy was finishing the last of the harnesses, helped by the footman. Levering myself up on the seat, I watched through the window as the footman hastily transferred all the gear on the gray to the last waiting horse, and then the Marquis swung into the saddle, leaning down to address a few words to the footman. Then the gray was led out of sight, and without any warning the carriage gave a great jolt and we started off.

Not one of the passersby showed the least interest in the proceedings. I wondered if I had missed yet another chance at escape, but if I did yell for help, who knew what the partisanship of the Lumm merchants was? I might very well have gotten my mouth gagged for my pains.

This did not help my spirits any, for now that the immediate discomforts had eased, I realized again that I was sick. How could I effect an escape when I had as much spunk as a pot of overboiled noodles?

I lay back down on the pillows, and before long the warmth and swaying of the carriage sent me off to sleep.

———

When I woke the air was hot and stuffy, and I was immediately aware of being shut up in a small painted-canvas box. But before I could react with more than that initial flash of distress, I realized that the carriage had stopped. I struggled up, wincing against a thumping great headache, just as the door opened.

There was the Marquis, holding his hand out. I took it, making a sour face. At least, I thought as I recognized an innyard, he looks as wind tousled and muddy as I must.

But there was no fanfare, no groups of gawking peasants and servants. He picked me up and carried me through a side door, and thence into a small parlor that overlooked the inn-yard. Seated on plain hemp-stuffed pillows, I looked out at the stable boy and driver busily changing the horses. The longshadows of late afternoon obscured everything; a cheap time-candle in a corner sconce marked the time as green-three.

Sounds at the door brought my attention around. An inn servant entered, carrying a tray laden with steaming dishes. As she set them out I looked at her face, wondering if I could get a chance to talk to her alone—if she might help a fellow-female being held prisoner?

"Coffee?" the Marquis said, splintering my thoughts.

I looked up, and I swear there was comprehension in those gray eyes.

"Coffee?" I repeated blankly.

"A drinkable blend, from the aroma." He tossed his hat and riding gloves onto the cushion beside him and leaned forward to pour a brown stream of liquid into two waiting mugs. "A miraculous drink. One of the decided benefits of our world-hopping mages," he said.

"Mages." I repeated that as well, trying to marshal my thoughts, which wanted to scamper, like frightened mice, in six different directions.

"Coffee. Horses." A careless wave toward the innyard.

67

"Chocolate. Kinthus. Laimun. Several of the luxuries that are not native to our world, brought here from others."

I could count the times we'd managed to get ahold of coffee, and I hadn't cared for its bitterness. But as I watched, honey and cream were spooned into the dark beverage, and when I did take a cautious sip, it was delicious. With the taste came warmth, a sense almost of well-being. For a short time I was content to sit, with my eyes closed, and savor the drink.

The welcome smell of braised potatoes and clear soup brought my attention back to the present. When I opened my eyes, there was the food, waiting before me.

"You had probably better not eat much more than that," said the Marquis. "We have a long ride ahead of us tonight, and you wouldn't want to regret your first good meal in days."

In weeks, I thought as I picked up a spoon, but I didn't say it out loud—it felt disloyal somehow.

Then the sense of what he'd said sank in, and I almost lost my appetite again. "How long to the capital?"

"We will arrive sometime tomorrow morning," he said.

I grimaced down at my soup, then braced myself up, thinking that I'd better eat, hungry or not, for I'd need my strength. "What is Galdran like?" I asked, adding sourly, "Besides being a tyrant, a coward, and a Covenant breaker?"

Shevraeth sat with his mug in his hands. He hadn't eaten much, but he was on his second cup of the coffee. "This is the third time you've brought that up," he said. "How do you know he intends to break the Covenant?"

"We have proof." I saw his eyes narrow, and I added in my hardest voice, "And don't waste your breath threatening me about getting it, because you won't. You really think I'd tell you what and where it is, just to have it destroyed? We may not be doing so well, but it seems my brother and I and our little untrained army are the only hope the Hill Folk have."

The Marquis was silent for a long pause, during which my

anger slowly evaporated, leaving me feeling more uncomfortable by the moment. I realized why just before he spoke: By refusing to tell him, I was implying that he, too, wanted to break the Covenant.

Well, doesn't he?—if he's allied with Galdran! I thought.

"To your question," the Marquis said, setting his cup down, " 'What is Galdran like?' By that I take it you mean, What kind of treatment can you expect from the King? If you take the time to consider the circumstances outside of your mountain life, you might be able to answer that for yourself." Despite the mild humor, the light, drawling voice managed somehow to sting. "The King has been in the midst of trade negotiations with Denlieff for over a year. You have cost him time and money that were better applied elsewhere. And a civil war never enhances the credit of the government in the eyes of visiting diplomats from the Empress in Cheras-al-Kherval, who does not look for causes so much as signs of slack control."

I dropped my spoon in the empty soup bowl. "So if he cracks down even harder on the people, it's all our fault, is that it?"

"You might contemplate, during your measures of leisure," he said, "what the purpose of a permanent court serves, besides to squander the gold earned by the sweat of the peasants' brows. And consider this: The only reason you and your brother have not been in Athanarel all along is because the King considered you too harmless to bother keeping an eye on." And with a polite gesture: "Are you finished?"

"Yes."

I was ensconced again in the carriage with my pillows and aching leg for company, and we resumed journeying.

The effect of the coffee was to banish sleep. Restless, angry with myself, angrier with my companion and with the unlucky happenstance that had brought me to this pass, I turned my thoughts once again to escape.

Clouds gathered and darkness fell very swiftly. When I could no longer see clearly, I hauled myself up and felt my way to the door. The only plan I could think of was to open the door, tumble out, and hopefully lose myself in the darkness. This would work only if no one was riding beside the carriage, watching.

A quick peek—a longer look—no one in sight.

I eased myself down onto the floor and then opened the door a crack, peering back. I was about to fling the door wider when the carriage lurched around a curve and the door almost jerked out of my hand. I half fell against the doorway, caught myself, and a moment later heard a galloping horse come up from behind the carriage.

I didn't look to see who was on it, but slammed the door shut and climbed back onto the seat.

And composed myself for sleep.

I knew I'd need it.

Noises and the dancing flickers and shadows of torchlight woke me once. The coach was still. I sat up, heard voices, lay down again. The headache was back, the fever—my constant companion for several days—high again. I closed my eyes and dropped into a tangle of nasty dreams.

When I woke, sunlight was streaming in the window. I sat up, feeling soggy and hot, but forgot my discomfort when I saw two armed and helmed soldiers in the brown and green of Galdran's army. Turning my head, I saw two more through the other window, and realized that at some point during the night we had picked up an escort.

Was this Shevraeth's attempt to bolster his prestige in front of the King? I was glad he hadn't deemed me worth impressing; the trip had been awful enough, but to have had to be stuck riding cross-country in the center of a pompous military formation would have been just plain humiliating.

Another glimpse through the window revealed we were passing buildings, and occasional knots of people and traffic, all drawn aside from the road to let us pass. Curious faces watched the cavalcade.

We had to be in Remalna-city. The idea made my stomach cramp up. Very soon they'd haul me out to my fate, and I knew I had to do my best not to disgrace our people.

For the first time—probably ever—I turned my thoughts to my appearance. There was nothing to be done about it, I thought dismally as I stared down at my clothes. Old, worn, bag-kneed woolen trousers, their dun color scarcely discernible for the splotches of mud and dried gore (on the left side). One scuffed, worn old moc and one filthy bare foot. The old brown tunic, once Bran's, was a mess, and my braid, which had come undone, looked like a thigh-length rattail. Hoping for the best, I spit on the underside of my tunic hem and scrubbed my face; the gritty feel did not bode well for success.

So I gave up. There was nothing for it but to keep my chin high, my demeanor as proud as possible; for after all, I had nothing to be ashamed of—outside of being caught in the first place. Our cause was right, those nasty cracks about mountain rabble and harmlessness notwithstanding.

I folded my arms across my front, ignoring the twinges and aches in my leg, tried to steady my breathing, and looked again out the window. It appeared we were drawing nearer to Athanarel, the royal palace, for the buildings were fewer and what I did see was designed to please the eye. Despite my disinclination, I was impressed. Ordered gardens, flower-banked canals, well-dressed people now decorated the view. A sweet carillon rang the change from gold to green: It was noon.

The carriage swept through two wrought-iron gates. I leaned forward and caught a glimpse of a high wall with sentries visible on it. Then we rolled down a tree-lined avenue to a huge flagged court before the biggest building I had ever seen.

The coach slowed. A moment later the door opened.

"Countess," someone unfamiliar said.

Feeling hot and cold at once, I slid from my pillow seat to the floor of the carriage and pushed my left leg carefully out, followed by my right. Then, sitting in the doorway, I looked up at two enormous soldiers, who reached down and took hold of my arms, one each. Positioned between them in a tight grip, I could make a pretense of walking.

They fell in the midst of two rows of guards, all of whom seemed to have been selected for their height and breadth. *To make me look ridiculous?* I thought, and forced my chin up proudly.

Remember, you are Meliara Astiar of Tlanth, your mother was descended from the greatest of Remalna's royal families, and you're about to face a tyrant and a thief, I told myself firmly. Whatever happened, whatever I said, might very well get carried back to Branaric. I owed it to the people at home not to rug-crawl to this villain.

So I exhorted myself as we progressed up a broad, sweeping marble stair. Two magnificent doors were flung open by flunkies in livery more fabulous than anything anyone in Tlanth—of high degree or low—had ever worn in my lifetime, and *klunk-klunk-klunk*, the rhythmic thud of boot heels impacted the marble floor of a great hall. High carved beams supported a distant ceiling. Windows filled with colored glass were set just under the roof, and beneath them hung flags—some new, some ancient. Under the flags, scattered along the perimeter of the marble floor, stood an uncountable number of people bedecked in silks and jewels. They stared at me in silence.

At some unseen signal the long line of guards around me stopped and their spears thudded to the floor with a noise that sounded like doom.

Then a tall figure with a long black cloak walked past us, plumed and coroneted helm carried in his gloved right hand. For a moment I didn't recognize the Marquis; somewhere along the way he'd gotten rid of his anonymous clothing and was now clad in a long black battle tunic, Remalna's crowned sun stitched on its breast. At his side hung his sword; his hair was braided back. He passed by without so much as a glance at me. His eyes were slack lidded, his expression bored.

He stopped before a dais, on which was a throne made of carved wood—a piece of goldwood so beautifully veined with golds and reds and umbers it looked like fire—and bowed low.

I was tempted to try hopping on my one good foot in order to get a glimpse of the enemy on the throne, but I didn't—and a moment later was glad I hadn't, for I saw the flash of a ring as Galdran waved carelessly at the guards. The four in front promptly stepped to each side, affording a clear field of vision between the King and me. I saw a tall, massively built man whose girth was running to portliness. Long red hair with gems braided into it, large nose, large ears, high forehead, pale blue eyes. He wore a long, carefully cultivated mustache. His mouth stretched in a cruel smile.

"So you won your wager, Shevraeth, eh?" he said. The tone was jovial, but there was an ugly edge to the voice that scared me.

"As well, Your Majesty," the Marquis drawled. "The dirt, the stretches of boredom . . . really, had it taken two days more, I could not have supported it, much as I'd regret the damage to my reputation for reneging on a bet."

Galdran fingered his mustache, then waved at me. "Are you certain someone hasn't been making a game of you? That looks like a scullery wench."

"I assure you, Your Majesty, this is Lady Meliara Astiar, Countess of Tlanth."

Galdran stepped down from his dais and came within about five paces of me, and looked me over from head to heels. The cruel smile widened. "I never expected much of that half-mad old man, but this is really rich!" He threw back his head and laughed.

And from all sides of the room laughter resounded up the walls, echoing from the rafters.

When it had died, Galdran said, "Cheer up, wench. You'll have your brother soon for company, and your heads will make a nice matched set over the palace gates." Once again he went off into laughter, and he gestured to the guards to take me away.

I opened my mouth to yell a parting insult but I was jerked to one side, which hurt my leg so much all I could do was gasp for breath. The echoes of the Court's laughter followed into the plain-walled corridor that the soldiers took me down, and then a heavy steel door slammed shut, and there was no sound beyond the marching of the guard and my own harsh breathing.

NINE

THE CELL I WAS LOCKED INTO SEEMED ESPECIALLY selected for its gloom and dampness.

I didn't hear any other victims in any of the surrounding cells, and I wondered if they'd put me squarely in the center of an empty wing. I could hear every noise down the corridor, for the dungeon seemed to be made of stone, save only the door, which was age-hardened wood with a grilled window. The cell's furniture consisted of a narrow and rickety rusty iron cot with rotten straw-stuffed ticking inadequately covering its few slats. In the corner was an equally rusty metal jug half filled with stale water.

Opposite the door was a smaller window set high up in the wall of the cell. Even without the grating, a cat would have had difficulty squeezing through the opening. The grating didn't keep out the occasional spurts of dust that clouded in, kicked up by passing horses or marching guards. I wondered if the window were set at ground level, which would bring a spouting of water onto me at the next rain. It certainly didn't keep out the cold.

The day wore on, marked only by subtle changes in the gloomy light in the cell, and by the distant sound of time-change bells. By its end I almost wished I *had* been handed off to the torturers, for at least after the inevitable interval of unimaginable nastiness I would have been more or less insensate.

Instead, what happened was a kind of refined torture that I hadn't expected: People came, in twos and threes and fours, to stare at me. The first time it happened I didn't know what to expect— except for those possible torturers—and I lay on the narrow, blanketless cot with my back to the door, my hands sweating.

But the door didn't open. Instead I heard the murmur of sing-song, pleasingly modulated voices, and then the titter of young women.

I kept my back to the door, glad they could not see my crimson face.

At the end of the day, after countless repeats of the curiosity-in-the-cage treatment, I wondered why Galdran had bothered to have me locked up at all, if he was permitting half the Court to troop down to gawk at me.

The answer came the next day. I might have understood it sooner, but by then the dampness and my continual fever had made it hard to think of much beyond my immediate surroundings. When the door first opened, I didn't turn around, and other than a flash of fear, I didn't really react.

Someone prodded me in the shoulder, and when I turned a grim-faced guard said, "Drink it. Fast." She held out a battered metal-handled mug.

Surprised, I took the mug, smelled a soup whose main component seemed to be cabbage. By then cabbage smelled more delicious than any meal in memory, and I downed the lukewarm soup with scarcely a pause for breath. The soldier grabbed the mug from my hands and went out, locking the door hastily.

Not too long after, another one came in, this time with a mug of tea, which I also had to gulp down. I did—and happily, too. Then, just after dark, two soldiers came, both standing in the doorway holding torches while a healer—an elderly man this time— with practiced haste unwrapped the bandage on my leg. Much as it hurt, I knew I needed a change, so I gritted my way through. I couldn't look at my own flesh, but kept my gaze on his face. His lips were pruned in heavy disapproval, and he shook his head now and then but didn't speak until he was done.

"The keem leaves have kept infection out," he murmured, "but it's not healing. Have you fever?"

"My closest companion," I said hoarsely—and realized it had been two days since I'd spoken.

"You'll need an infusion of willow bark..." He stopped, grabbed up the mess with a quick swipe of his hand, then left without another word.

The throbbing was just settling into a dull ache when the door opened again, and this time a completely new soldier came in, bearing a mug and a bundle under his arm. The bundle was a blanket, and the steam from the mug smelled familiar... At the first refreshingly bitter sip I realized that here was my infusion of willow bark, and it finally sank into my fevered brain that Galdran probably didn't know about any of this. What I had experienced for the past two days, from the gawks to the gifts, were the effects of bribery. Those Court people paid to get a look at me—and, it seemed, some had for whatever reason bought me what comfort they could.

Bribery! If things could come in, couldn't something go out? Something like me? Except I had nothing at all to bribe anyone with. And I suspected that the going price for smuggling somebody out would be a thumping great sum beyond whatever anyone had paid to slip me a cup of soup.

A half-hysterical bubble of laughter tried to fight its way up from somewhere inside me, but I controlled it, afraid once I began I might start wailing like a wolf when it sees the moons.

After a short time the willow did its work upon me, and I fell into the first good sleep I'd had in days.

Sleep ended abruptly the next morning when the cell door opened and my blanket was unceremoniously snatched off me. Within a short space I was shivering again, but I did feel immeasurably better than I had. Even my foot ached a bit less.

That day it rained, and the window leaked. Ignoring the twinges in my foot, I dragged my cot away, which was a mistake because its legs promptly collapsed. I sat on it anyway, more or less out of the wet.

More gifts that day: some hot stew, more tea, and a castoff tunic that smelled of mildew and was much too large, but I pulled it on gratefully. At night, another blanket, which disappeared the next morning—this time with an apologetic murmur from the guard who removed it.

The gifts helped, but not enough to counteract the cold or my own state of health. Somewhere in the third or fourth day infection must have set in, for the intermittent fever that had plagued me from the start mounted into a bone-aching, chill-making burner.

I was sicker than I'd ever been in a short but healthy life, so sick I couldn't sleep but lay watching imaginary bugs crawl up the walls. And of course it had to be while I was like this—just about the lowest I'd sunk yet—that the Marquis of Shevraeth chose to reappear in my life.

It was not long after the single bell toll that means midnight and first-white-candle. Very suddenly the door opened, and a tall, glittering figure walked in, handing something to the silent guard at the door, who then went out. I heard footsteps receding as I stared, without at first comprehending, at the torch-bearing aristocrat before me.

I blinked at the resplendent black and crimson velvet embroidered over with gold and set with rubies, and at the rubies glittering on fingers and in pale braided hair. My gaze rose to the rakish hat set low over the familiar gray eyes.

He must have been waiting for me to recognize him.

"The King will summon you at first-green tomorrow," the Marquis said quickly, all trace of the drawl gone. "It appears that your brother has been making a fool of Debegri, leading him all over your mountains and stealing our horses and supplies. The King has changed his mind: Either you surrender, speaking for your brother and your people, or he's going to make an example of you in a public execution tomorrow. Not a noble's death, but a criminal's."

"Criminal's?" I repeated stupidly, my voice nearly gone.

"It will last all day," he said with a grimace of distaste. It was the first real expression I'd ever seen from him, but by then I was in no mood to appreciate it.

Sheer terror overwhelmed me then. All my courage, my firm resolves, had worn away during the time-measures of illness, and I could not prevent my eyes from stinging with tears of fear—and shame. "Why are you telling me this?" I said, hiding my face in my hands.

"Will you consider it? It might . . . buy you time."

This made no sense to me. "What time can I buy with dishonor?" All I could imagine was the messengers flying westward, and the looks on Bran's and Khesot's faces—and on Julen's and Calaub's and Devan's, people who had risked their lives twice trying to rescue me—when they found out. "I know why you're here." I snuffled into my palms. "Want to gloat? See me turn coward? Well, gloat away . . ." But I couldn't say anything more, and after about as excruciating a pause as I'd ever endured, I heard his heels on the stone.

The door shut, the footsteps withdrew, and I was left in silence.

It was *then* that I hit the low point of my life.

I don't know how long I had been sniffing and snorting there on my broken bunk (and I didn't care who heard me) when I became aware of furtive little sounds from the corridor. Nothing loud—no more than a slight scrape—then a soft grunt of surprise.

I looked up, saw nothing in the darkness.

A voice whispered, "Countess?"

A voice I recognized. "Azmus!"

"It is I," he whispered. "Quickly—before they figure out about the doors."

"What?"

"I've been shadowing this place for two days, trying to figure a way in," he said as he eased the door open. "There must be something going on. The outer door wasn't locked tonight, and neither is this one."

"Shevraeth," I croaked.

"What?"

"Marquis of Shevraeth. Was here gloating at me. The guard must have expected him to lock it, since the grand Marquis sent the fellow away," I muttered as I got shakily to my feet. "And he —being an aristocrat, and above mundane things—probably assumed the guard would lock it. *Uh!* Sorry, I just can't walk—"

At once Azmus sprang to my side. Together we moved out of the corridor, me hating myself for not even *thinking* of trying the door—except, how could I have gotten anywhere on my own?

At the end of the corridor a long shape lay still on the ground. Unconscious or dead, I didn't know, and I wasn't going to check. I just hoped it wasn't one of the nice guards.

Outside it was raining in earnest, which made visibility difficult for our enemies as well as for us. Azmus took a good grip on me, breathing into my ear: "Brace up—we'll have to move fast."

The trip across the courtyard was probably fifty paces or so, but it seemed fifty days' travel to me. Every step was a misery, but I managed, heartened by the reflection that each step took me farther from that dungeon and—I hoped fervently—from the fate in store if Galdran got his claws into me again.

We went through a discreet side door in a low, plain side building. Lamps glowed at intervals on the walls, seeming unnaturally bright to my dark-accustomed, feverish eyes. Breathing harshly, Azmus led the way down the hall and up some narrow stairs to a small room.

As soon as the door was shut he touched a glowglobe on a table, and in its faint bluish light, he sprang to a long cupboard and yanked it open. Shelves and shelves of folded cloth were revealed. "Here," he said. "Put this on, my lady. Quickly—make haste, make haste. We can get through the grounds as servants only if a search is not raised."

I held up what he had handed me and saw a gown. It was much too wide. As I looked at it rather helplessly, he bit his lip, his round face concerned; then he grabbed it back and pulled something else out. "There. That's for a stable hand, but it ought to fit better— they are mostly young."

I realized he was already wearing the livery of a palace servant. Not the fabulous livery of the foot servants who waited on the nobles in the palace, but the plain garb of the underservants. Short, stocky, with an unprepossessing face, Azmus was easily overlooked in any crowd. I didn't know his age, and it was impossible to guess from his snub-nosed face, all of which made him the perfect spy.

Wincing, I pulled off the mildewed tunic some unknown benefactor had gifted me with, and I yanked the livery over my filthy, rumpled clothes. I left my braid inside the tunic, pulled a cap on, and shoved my feet into a pair of shoes that were much too big. The tunic came down to just below my knees. We both looked at my trousers, which were not unlike the color of the stable hands', and he said with a pained smile: "In the dark, you'll pass. And our only hope of making it is now, while no one can see us." He bundled my mildewed tunic and my one moc under his own clothes.

"Where are we going?" I asked as he helped me down the stairs.

"Stable. One chance of getting out is there—if we're fast."

Neither of us wasted any more breath. He had to look around constantly while bearing my weight. I concentrated on walking.

At the stable, servants were running back and forth on errands, but we made our way slowly along the wall of a long, low building toward a row of elegant town carriages.

I murmured, "Don't tell me ... I'm to steal one of these?"

Azmus gave a breathless laugh. "You'll steal a ride—if we can get you in. Your best chance is the one that belongs to the Princess of Renselaeus—if we can, by some miracle, get near it. The guards will never stop it, even if the hue and cry is raised. And she doesn't live within Athanarel, but at the family palace in the city."

"Renselaeus ..." I repeated, then grinned. The Princess was the mother of the Marquis. The Prince, her husband, who was rumored to have been badly wounded in the Pirate Wars, never left their land. I loved the idea of making my escape under the nose of Shevraeth's mother. Next thing to snapping my fingers under *his* nose.

Suddenly there was an increase in noise from the direction of the palace. A young girl came running toward us, torch hissing and streaming in the rain. "Savona!" she yelled. "Savona!"

A carriage near the front of the line was maneuvered out, rolling out of the courtyard toward the distant great hall.

Keeping close to the walls, we moved along the line until we were near a handsome equipage that looked comfortable and well sprung, even in the dark and rain. All around it stood a cluster of servants dressed in sky blue, black, and white.

Two more names were called out by runners, and then came, "Renselaeus!"

But before the carriage could roll, the runner dashed up and said, "Wait! Wait! Get canopies! She won't come out without canopies—says her gown will be ruined."

One of the servants groaned; they all, except the driver, dashed inside the stable.

Next to me, Azmus drew in his breath in a sharp hiss. "Come," he said. "This is it."

And we crossed the few steps to the carriage. A quick look. Everyone else was seeing to their own horses, or wiping rain from windows, or trying to stay out of the worst of the wet. At the back of the coach was a long trunk; Azmus lifted the lid and helped me climb up and inside. "I do not know if I can get to the Renselaeus palace to aid you," he warned as he lowered the lid.

"I'll make it," I promised. "Thanks. You'll be remembered for this."

"Down with Merindar," he murmured. "Farewell, my lady."

And the lid closed.

Lying flat was a relief, though the thick-woven hemp flooring scraped at my cheek. Around me muffled voices arrived. The carriage rocked as the foot servants grabbed hold. Then we moved, slowly, smoothly. Then stopped.

Faintly, beckoning and lovely, I heard two melodic lines traded back and forth between sweet wind instruments, and the thrumming of metallic harp strings.

A high, imperious voice drowned the music: "Come, come! Closer together! Step as one, now. I mustn't ruin this gown...The King himself spoke in praise of it...I can only wear it again if it is not ruined...Step lively there, and have a care for puddles. There!"

I could envision a crowd of foot servants holding rain canopies over her head, like a moving tent, as the old lady bustled across the mud. She arrived safely in the carriage, and when she was closed in, once again we started to roll.

"Ware, gate!" the driver called presently. "Ware for Renselaeus!" The carriage scarcely slowed. I heard the creak of the great iron gates—the ones that were supposed to be sporting my head within a day. They swung shut with a *graunch*ing of protesting metal, and the carriage rolled out of Athanarel and into the city.

My next worry, of course, was how to get out of the trunk without being discovered. I'd seen how busily all those servants cleaned their carriages as they waited in the rain, so I knew the first thing the Renselaeus lackeys would want to do the moment they stopped would be to rub the elegantly painted canvas with rainproofing wax polish. Would that mean opening the luggage trunk? My heart was pounding loud enough to be heard at the palace, it seemed to me, when we finally came to a halt.

And then came the imperious voice again; I'd discounted the vanity of an old lady. "No, no, leave that. Where are my canopies? Take me across the yard. Come, come, don't dawdle!"

Footsteps moved away, and I knew I had to move right then— or risk discovery.

Shouldering the lid up, I eased out, falling to the straw-covered ground when I tried to step on my left foot. A few paces away I saw a pitchfork leaning against a wall. Hauling myself to my feet, with my heart still thumping somewhere near my throat, I lunged my way across to the pitchfork, steadied myself on it, and used it as a brace for my left leg.

A quick look either way, then I was out the stable door, into a narrow alley. I hobbled into its welcome gloom, turned the first moment I could, and kept moving until I was thoroughly lost and soaked right to the skin. By then my hands were sore from the pitchfork's rusty metal, and my racing heart had slowed. It was time to find a place to hide, and rest, and plan my next move.

I was on a broad street, which was dangerous enough. As yet there was still some traffic, but soon that would be gone.

Light and noise drew my attention. Farther down, my street intersected another. On the corner was a great inn, its stableyard lit by glowglobes. As I watched, a loaded coach-and-six slowly lumbered in. Stable hands ran out and surrounded it. I hobbled my way along the wall, then stepped into the courtyard. At the side was a great mound of hay covered by a slanting roof. What a perfect bed that would be! My body was, by then, one great ache, and I longed to stretch out and sleep and sleep and sleep.

I kept my eyes on the hay. Every other step I moved my pitch-fork around, as though tidying the yard. No one paid me the least heed as I stepped closer, closer—

"Boy! You there!"

I turned, my heart slamming.

The innkeeper stood on a broad step, his apron covering a brawny chest. Nearby a soberly dressed man wearing the hat of a prosperous farmer dismounted from a fine mare. "Boy—girl? Here, take this gentleman's horse," the innkeeper said, snapping his fingers at me.

Trying not to be obvious about my pitchfork crutch, I stepped slowly nearer, toward the light. Warmth and food smells wafted out from a cheerfully noisy common room. Clearly this inn never knew quiet, night or day.

"Hey, is that palace livery? A palace hand, are you? What you doing here?"

"Errand," I said, trying desperately to make up a story.

But that appeared to be good enough. "Look, you, our hands are busy. You trim down this horse and put him with the hacks, and there'll be a hot toddy waiting inside for ye. How's that?"

I ducked my head in the nod that I'd seen the stable hands use at the palace. The man standing next to the innkeeper surrendered the reins to me and pulled off the saddlebags, yawning hugely as he did. "Wet season ahead, Master Kepruid," he said, following the innkeeper inside. "I know the signs . . ."

And I was left there, holding a horse by the reins.

My inner debate lasted about the space of one breath. I looked at the mare, which was as wet as I but otherwise seemed fine; she had not been galloped into exhaustion.

So I led the mare back toward the entry to the stable, my shoulder blades feeling as if a hundred unfriendly eyes watched. Then I leaned against her, standing on my bad foot, which almost gave out. I hopped up—ignoring the sharp pain—and grabbed the saddle horn, throwing my good leg over the saddle. . . . And I was mounted!

The pitchfork dropped; I gathered the reins and nudged the animal's sides. She sidled, tossed her head, nickered softly—and then began to move.

Several streets later, I kicked off the awful shoes, and when we had left the last of the houses of Remalna-city behind I decided I'd better get rid of the palace livery in case everyone around recognized it. I was so wet there was no chance of being warm—the tunic was merely extra weight on me. Gladly I pulled it off and balled it up, and when we crossed a bridge topped with glowglobes, I dropped my burden into a thicket near the water's edge.

So . . . where to go, besides west?

My body needed rest, warmth, sleep; but my spirit longed for home. Once I'd left the city and the last of what light there was, I could see nothing of the rain-swept countryside. The horse moved steadily toward the western mountains, which were discernible only as a blacker line against the faintly glowing sky. Gradually, without realizing it, I relinquished to the mare the choice of direction and struggled just to keep awake, to stay on her back.

After an interminable ride I tried lying along her neck. Beneath the rain-cold mane her muscles moved, and faint warmth radiated into me. I drifted in and out of dreams and wakefulness until the dream images overlay reality like dye-prints on silk. Looking back, I realize I'd slipped into delirium; but at the time I thought I was managing to hold on to consciousness, only that my perception of the world had gradually diminished to the fire in my leg and the rough horse hair beneath my cheek.

Dawn was just starting to lift the darkness when the mare walked into a farmyard and stopped, lifting her head.

I gripped weakly at her mane with both fists to keep myself from falling, and I sat up. The world swam sickeningly. Somewhere was the golden light of a window, and the sound of a door opening, and then voices exclaiming.

"Heyo, Mama, Drith is back—but there's someone else on her instead of Papa." And then a sharp voice: "Who are you?"

I opened my mouth, but no sound came out. The whirl of the universe had increased, and it drew me inexorably into the vortex of welcoming darkness.

TEN

W HEN I FIRST OPENED MY EYES—AND IT TOOK
about as much effort as had the entire escape from Athanarel—
someone made me drink something. I think I fell asleep again in
the midst of swallowing.

Then I slept, and dreamed, and slept some more. I woke again
when someone coaxed me into a bath. I remember the delicious
sense of warm water pouring over my skin, and afterward the clean
smell of fresh sheets, and myself in a soft nightgown.

Another time I roused to the lilting strains of music. I thought
I was back at the palace, and though I wanted to go closer, to hear
the sound more clearly, I knew I ought to get away.... I stirred
restlessly ... and the music stopped.

I slept again.

Waking to the sound of the bells for third-gold, I found myself
staring up at a pair of interested brown eyes.

"She's awake!" my watcher called over her shoulder. Then she
turned back to me and grinned. She had a pointed face, curly dark
hair escaping from two short braids, and a merry voice as she said,
"Splat!" She clapped her hands lightly. "We were fair guffered
when you toppled right off Drith, facedown in the chickenyard
mud. Lucky it was so early, for no one was about but us."

I winced.

She grinned again. "You're either the worst horse thief in the entire kingdom, or else you're that missing countess. Which is it?"

"Ara." The voice of quiet reproach came from the doorway.

I lifted my eyes without moving my head, saw a matron of pleasant demeanor and comfortable build come into the room bearing a tray.

Ara jumped up. She seemed a couple years younger than I. "Let me!"

"Only if you promise not to pester her with questions," the mother replied. "She's still much too ill."

Ara shrugged, looking unrepentant. "But I'm dying to know."

The mother set the tray down on a side table and smiled down at me. She had the same brown eyes as her daughter, but hers were harder to read. "Can you sit up yet?"

"I can try," I said hoarsely.

"Just high enough so's we can put these pillows behind you." Ara spoke over her shoulder as she dashed across the room.

My head ached just to watch her, and I closed my eyes again.

"Ara."

"Mama! I didn't do *anything*!"

"Patience, child. You can visit with her next time, when she's stronger. If she likes," the woman amended, which gave me a pretty good idea they knew which of the two choices I was. *So much for a story*, I thought wearily.

In complete silence the mother helped me by lifting my cup for me to sip from, and by buttering bread then cutting it small so I wouldn't have to tear it. Soon, my stomach full, my body warm, I slid back into sleep.

The next time I woke it was morning. Clear yellow light slanted in an open window, making the embroidered curtains wave in and out in slow, graceful patterns. I lay without moving, watching with sleepy pleasure.

I might have drifted off again when there was a quick step, and Ara appeared, this time with pink blooms stuck in her braids. "You're awake," she said happily. "Do you feel better?"

"Lots," I said. My voice was stronger.

"I'll tell Mama, and you'll have breakfast in a wink." She whirled out in a flash of embroidered skirts, then bobbed back into view. Lowering her voice as she knelt by the bed-shelf, she said, "Feel like talking?"

She sounded so conspiratorial I felt the urge to smile, though I don't think the impulse made it all the way to my face.

"That thing on your ankle was pret-ty nasty. Lucky we have keem leaves, and herbs from Grandma. Mama thought you were going to die." Ara grimaced. "At first Papa was mad about the horse, for he had to pay out all his profits to hire another, plus the bother of returning it, but he didn't want you to die, nor even want to report you—not after the first day. And not after we *Found Out.*" The last two words were uttered in a tone of vast importance, her eyes rounding. "Luz will tell you he heard it first, but it was I who went to the Three Rings and listened to the gossip."

I swallowed. "Luz?"

She rolled her eyes. "My brother. He's ten. Horrid age!"

I thought of Branaric, who had always been my hero. Had he ever thought I was at a horrid age? A complex of emotions eddied through me. When I looked up at Ara again, she had her lower lip between her teeth.

"I'm sorry," she said. "Have I spoken amiss?"

"No." I tried a smile. It felt false, but she seemed relieved.

The mother came in then, carrying another tray. "Good morning. Is there anything you wish for?"

"Just to thank you," I said. "The—horse. I, um, didn't think about theft. I just . . . needed to get out of Remalna-city."

"Well, she brought you right home." The mother's eyes crinkled with amusement. "I think the hardest thing was my spouse having to endure being chaffed at the inn for losing Drith. He—we—decided against mentioning the theft to anyone as yet."

I tried to consider what that meant, and failed. Something must have showed in my face, because she said quickly, "Fret not. No one has said anything, and no one will, without your leave. There's time enough to talk when you are feeling stronger."

I sighed. And after a good breakfast, I did feel a great deal stronger. Also, for the first time, I didn't just slip back into sleep. Ara, hovering about, said, "Would you like to sit on my balcony? It faces away from the farm, so no one can see you. I have a garden—it's my own. All the spring blooms are out. Of course," she hastened to add, "it's just a farm garden, not like any palace or anything."

"I haven't had a garden since my mother died. I'd like to see yours very much."

"Try walking," Ara said briskly, her cheeks pink with pleasure. "Mama thinks you should be able to now, for your ankle's all scabbed over and no bones broke, though they might be bruised. Here's my arm if you need it."

I swung my legs out and discovered that my hair, clean and sweet smelling, had been combed out and rebraided into two shining ropes.

Standing up, I felt oddly tall, but the familiar ache had dulled to a bearable extent, and I walked without much difficulty from the small room onto a wide balcony. A narrow wicker bench there was already lined with pillows. I sank down and looked out over a blooming garden. Through some sheltering trees, I glimpsed part of the house, and a bathhouse, and gently rolling hillocks planted closely in crop rows. And beyond, purple in the distance, the mountains. My mountains.

"This is the best view." Ara waved her arms proudly. "I tried it from several rooms. See, the roses are there, and the climbing vine makes a frame, and ferris ferns add green here..."

"Ara, don't chatter her ear off." The mother appeared behind us. "Here's another cup of listerblossom tea. I don't think you can drink too much of it," she added, putting it into my hands.

I thanked her and sipped. Ara stayed quiet for the space of two swallows, then said, "Do you like my garden?"

"I do," I said. "Moonflowers are my favorite—especially that shade of blue. They mostly grow white up in our mountains."

"We have only blue here. Though I'm getting slips of some that grow pale lavender at the center, and purple out." She sat back, her profile happy. "I love the thought that I will be able to sit my whole life on this balcony and look out at my garden."

"You're the heir?" I asked.

She nodded, not hiding her pride. Then, turning a round gaze on me she said, "And you really are the Countess of Tlanth?"

I nodded.

She closed her eyes and sighed. "Emis over on Nikaru Farm is going to be *soooo* jealous when she finds out. She thinks she's so very fine a lady, just because she has a cousin in service at Athanarel and her brother in the Guard. There *is* no news from Athanarel if *she* doesn't know it first, or more of it than anyone."

"What is the news?" I asked, feeling the old fear close round me.

She pursed her lips. "Maybe Mama is right about my tongue running like a fox in the wild. Are you certain you want all this now?"

"Very much," I said.

"It comes to this: The Duke of Savona and the Marquis of Shevraeth have another wager, on which one can find you first. The King thinks it great sport, and they have people on all the main roads leading west to the mountains."

"Did they say anything about my escape?"

She shook her head. "Luz overheard some merchants at the Harvest—that's the inn down the road at Garval—saying they thought it was wizard work or a big conspiracy. I went with Papa when he returned to the Three Rings in Remalna-city, and everyone was talking about it." She grinned. "Elun Kepruid—he's the innkeeper's son at Three Rings, and he likes me plenty—was telling

91

me all the *real* gossip from the palace. The King was very angry, and at first wanted to execute all the guards who had duty the night you got out, except the ones he really wanted had disappeared, and everyone at Court thought there was a conspiracy, and they were afraid of attack. But then the lords started the wagers and turned it all into a game. Savona swore he'd fling you at the King's feet inside of two weeks. Baron Debegri, who was just returned from the mountains, said he'd bring your head—then take it and fling it at your brother's feet. He's a hard one, the Baron, Emis's brother said." She grimaced. "Is this too terrible to hear?"

"No . . . No. I just need . . . to think."

She put her chin on her hands. "Did you see the Duke?"

"Which duke?"

"Savona." She sighed. "Emis *has* seen him—twice. She gets to visit her cousin at Winter Festival. She says he's even *more* handsome than I can imagine. Four duels . . . Did you?"

I shook my head. "All I saw was the inside of my cell. And the King. And that Shevraeth," I added somewhat bitterly.

"He's supposed to have a head for nothing but clothes. And gambling." Ara shrugged dismissively. "Everybody thinks it's really Debegri who—well, got you."

"What got me was a trap. And it was my own fault."

She opened her mouth, then closed it. "Mama says I ought not to ask much about what happened. She says the less I know, the less danger there is to my family. You think that's true?"

Danger to her family. It was a warning. I nodded firmly. "Just forget it, and I'll make you a promise. If I live through this mess, and things settle down, I'll tell you everything. How's that?"

Ara clapped her hands and laughed. "That's nacky! *Especially* if you tell me all about your palace in Tlanth. *How* Emis's nose will turn purple from envy—when I can tell her, that is!"

I thought of our old castle, with its broken windows and walls, the worn, shabby furnishings and overgrown garden, and sighed.

After a time Ara had to do her chores, leaving me on the porch with a fresh infusion of tea to drink, her garden to look at, and her words to consider.

Not that I got very far. There were too many questions. Like: Where did those guards go? Azmus had overcome one, but I didn't remember having seen any more. Then there were the unlocked doors. The one to my cell could be explained away, but not the outside one. If there was a conspiracy, was Azmus behind it? Or someone else—and if so, who; and more importantly, to what end?

It was just possible that those dashing aristos had contrived my escape for a game, just as a cruel cat will play with a mouse before the kill. Their well-publicized bet could certainly account for that. The wager would also serve very nicely as a warning to ordinary people not to interfere with their prey, I thought narrowly.

Which meant that if I'd left any clue to my trail, I had better move on. Soon.

While considering all this I fell asleep again with the half-filled mug in my lap. When I woke the sun was setting and my hands were empty. A clean quilt lay over me. Somewhere someone was playing music: the steel strings of a tiranthe, and a pipe. I listened to a wild melody that made me wish I could get up and dance among Ara's flowers, followed by a ballad so sad I was thrown back in memory to the days after my mother died.

It was during the third song that two quiet figures came out onto the balcony. The man I recognized after a moment as the one who had handed me his horse's reins that night an age ago. He set down a lamp and sat in a wicker chair nearby. His wife brought me more tea, then took her place in another chair.

The man said, "Are you well enough to discuss plans, my lady?"

"Of course." I sat up straight. "I'm in your debt. What can I do?"

He looked over at his wife, who said quietly, "Master Kepruid remembers the stable hand from the palace who was supposed to do for Drith. He has said nothing about our story of the dropped reins and the need to hire a horse to chase a mare who has made

93

the trip into the city every month for six years. And he won't, if you can promise you won't carry your war into the city."

"Carry my war," I repeated, feeling a cold wash of unpleasantness through me. "It—it isn't *my* war."

"Yours and the Count of Tlanth's," the man said. "We understand that much."

"Then . . . you are content under Galdran Merindar?" I asked.

"Am I?" the man said. "I am content enough. The merchants in the city buy goods from our village, and I receive my portion of their profits for arranging the selling, which covers our taxes. The farm does just well enough to keep us fed. If the taxes do not rise too steeply again, we will manage. I cannot answer for others."

The mother said, "Rumor has it your war is intended to protect the Covenant, but the King insists it was you who was going to break it. Rumor also has it you and your brother said you were going to war for the betterment of Remalna."

"It's true, I assure you," I said. "I mean, about our going to war for the Covenant. The King intends to break it—we have proof of that. And we *do* want to help the kingdom."

"Perhaps it is true." The mother gave me a serious look. "But you must consider our position. Too many of us remember what life was like on the coast during the Pirate Wars. No matter who holds a port, or a point, it is our lands, and houses, that get burned, our food taken for supplies, our youths killed. And sometimes not just the youths. We could have a better king, but not at the cost of our towns and farms being laid waste by contending armies."

These words, so quietly spoken, astounded me. I thought of my entire life, devoted to the future, in which I would fight for the freedom of just such people as these. Would it all be a waste?

"And if he does raise the taxes again? I know he has four times in the last ten years."

"Then we will manage somehow." The man shook his head. "And mayhap the day will come when war is necessary, but we want to put that day off as long as we can; for when it does come, it will not be so lightly recovered from. Can you see that?"

I thought of the fighting so far. Who had died while trying to rescue me? Those people would never see the sun set again.

"Yes. I do see it." I looked up and saw them both watching me anxiously.

The woman leaned forward and patted my hand. "As he says, we do not speak for everyone."

But the message was clear enough. And I could see the justice of it. For had I not taken these people's mare without a thought to the consequences? Just so could I envision an army trampling Ara's garden, their minds filled with thoughts of victory, their hearts certain they were in the right.

"Then how do we address the wrongs?" I asked, and was ashamed at the quiver in my voice.

"That I do not know," the man said. "I concern myself with what is mine, and I try to help my neighbors. The greater questions—justice, law, and the rights and obligations of power—those seem to be the domain of you nobles. You have the money, and the training, and the centuries of authority."

Unbidden, Shevraeth's voice returned to mind, that last conversation before the journey into Remalna, *You might contemplate during your measures of leisure what the purpose of a permanent court serves . . . And consider this: The only reason you and your brother have not been in Athanarel all along is because the King considered you too harmless to bother keeping an eye on.*

I sighed. "And at least three of the said aristocrats are busy looking for me. Maybe it's time I was on my way."

There was no mistaking the relief in their faces.

"I did the best I could with your clothes, but they did not survive washing," the woman said. "However, Ara has an old gown laid by. It's a very nice one, but she no longer fits into it."

"Anything," I said. "And I don't mind wearing my old clothes. A hole or two won't hurt me. Actually, I'm used to them."

She laughed. "I very much fear they disintegrated, or the tunic did, anyway. The trousers I bade Ara bury out in the turned field, for I knew there'd be no bringing those bloodstains out." She got to her feet. "Does Ara's music distress you anymore?"

"It never did." I looked at her in surprise. "I like it very much."

She gave me an odd, slightly troubled glance, then took my empty mug and led the way back to the little room I'd been sleeping in.

The next morning Ara seemed resigned about my leaving. She reminded me of my promise three times, then offered to brush out my hair for me. I agreed, sipping the last cup of their healing tea and wondering how far I'd get.

When she was done she flexed her fingers and stood back admiringly. "Knee-length hair! Not even Lady Tamara Chamadis— you know, daughter of the Countess of Turlee—has hair that long."

"I haven't cut it since my mother was killed. Swore I wouldn't until—well, she was avenged," I finished rather lamely, thinking of my conversation with her parents, who still had not told me their names, nor permitted their son or other dependents anywhere in my presence.

"Well, don't even then. It's the prettiest color in the world— not just brown, but brown and red and gold and wheat. Like the colorwoods!"

"My brother's is the same color." I figured that hair, at least, was a safe-enough topic. Pulling mine from long habit into separate strands, I braided it tightly as Ara chattered about the hair colors of her friends.

She opened a trunk and pulled out folded lengths of material. "Mother thought this one might fit. Put it on!"

I'd had my first real bath early that morning; I went to the bathhouse with Ara, wearing her mother's cloak, and no one had seen us. As I reached for the underdress, I realized how very reluctant I was to leave. Ara's parents wanted me gone. I needed to get home. But there was a strong part of me that would have been happy to sit in their garden and listen to music.

"It's a bit long, but you can kirtle it up." Ara looked me over critically.

The underdress was white linen, embroidered at the voluminous sleeves, the neck, and the hem with tiny crimson birds and flowers. The overdress was next, with a heavy skirt of robin's-egg blue, then the bodice, which laced up to a square neck that was old-fashioned but pleasing.

"There. 'Tis beautiful! Hoo, I've never had that small a waist, even when I was Luz's age." Using both hands, she brought out a long, narrow mirror and set it on the trunk, tipping it back.

I looked down, hardly recognizing the person staring back at me. She looked much older than I was used to looking: a bony face, large blue eyes that—I realized—matched the skirt of the gown. To myself I just looked thin, with a wary gaze, but Ara sighed with happy sentimentality. "You are so graceful, just like a bird. And beautiful!"

"Now, that I'm not," I said, half laughing and half exasperated.

"Well, not in the way of Lady Tamara, whose eyelashes are famous, and whose features get poems written on them, according to Emis. But it's the way your face changes..." She flipped her hands up.

I laughed again, feeling foolish. I realized that no one had commented on my appearance since I was small; I simply *was*. I certainly had not looked into a mirror for many seasons, and what clothing I had was chosen for freedom of wear, and for warmth.

She looked at me in blatant surprise. "Don't say—have you no flirts?"

"No." I shrugged. "Never have."

"Well." I could see her struggling not to think the less of me. "I've had them since I turned fifteen. Master Kepruid's son is just one! Makes the dances ever so much more fun." She shrugged and grinned again. "Mama doesn't want me twoing before my Flower Day, at the least. And in truth, her rule is not so hard, for it's nacky having lots of flirts. Emis thinks she's more popular than I am, with those cousins and all, but—"

The door hanging flapped open, and Ara blinked in surprise. I found myself reaching for a weapon at my belt, and of course there was none.

But no enemy came in, only a gangling boy just about my height. His round cheeks were flushed with exertion. Staring at me with frank curiosity, he said, "They're searching cross-country from the river west . . . Daro says that his brother in the Guard told them they found palace livery in the river."

Ara bit her lip. "We're more south than west."

"But it's close enough that I'd better go. Thank you, Luz," I said.

The boy grinned. "I better lope, or Mama'll have my hide. But I won't tweet, oak-vow!" He slapped his forearm and touched his brow, then he dashed out again.

I sighed. "If I can have one more thing—a hat—I do swear I'll repay you somehow, someday."

Ara giggled as she dived into the trunk; I realized then that I had been using her room. "I don't have an extra hat, for I've just begun to wear them, but you can take this." She held out a long fringed scarf with dancing animals and birds embroidered on it. "You look young enough to wear a kerchief. But don't tie it under your chin. Behind, like we do." With quick fingers, she fixed the scarf.

Ara's mother came in then, and her relief to find me dressed and ready to go was plain. "I don't think we have any shoes to fit you," she said.

"That's all right. I'm used to being barefoot, and in much colder weather than this."

They seemed surprised, but neither of them spoke as we walked out. It was the first time I had seen any of the house besides the bedroom. I glanced with great curiosity over a landing into a big central room with two stories of doors leading off it. In the center was a round ceramic stove tiled in colorful patterns—a very old house, then. Built before stoves with vents to rooms were built, but after the Hill Folk gave Remalna the Fire Spell; for people used to put their Fire Sticks in such rounded stoves, thinking the heat would go out in a circle.

We went down a narrow flight of stairs. The mother glanced quickly down two clean, shiny-floored hallways before gesturing me into a tiny storeroom. "My cousin, who does all the kitchen work, mustn't see you. He's a fine young man, but gabby. So all that tea has been for my feigned illness." She smiled wryly. "Here is some food—"

"Mama, that's an old basket," Ara protested. "Why don't you give her one of Sepik's nice ones?"

The mother hesitated, looking at me.

I said firmly, "Not if Sepik, whoever that is, makes baskets with a distinctive pattern. The old one will suit me much better."

I was handed a basket covered with a worn cloth. The weight of the basket was promising.

"Can I walk her to the hidey-path?" Ara asked.

"No. You are already late for your chores. I am going to take a walk for my health. Not a word more."

Ara pressed her lips together, winked at me, then fled.

I followed the mother through a side door. We walked down through the garden and beneath a pleasant copse of spreading trees. The land sloped away toward a stream, which wound its way through a tangle of growth. Through this a narrow footpath paralleled the stream.

She did not speak as we walked. I concentrated on keeping up with her brisk pace. My ankle, I was glad to find, only ached dully, and the skirt kept twigs and brush from touching my still-sensitive skin. I didn't know how I'd feel later, but thus far I was doing well enough to get off the farm with the haste they seemed to think necessary.

"Here's our border," she said, stopping suddenly. We stepped off the path, and she parted the hanging leaves of a willow to point at rounded hills with an ancient stone wall crossing them. It was low and worn, just tall enough to keep sheep in. "If you cross that way, you'll catch up with the path leading to Ruka-at-Nimm, which is a good-sized village. It's also well south of the Akaeriki road, which is the main one west."

"I'll take it from here. The closer I get to the mountains, the faster I know how to cross the terrain. I'm grateful to your family."

She pressed her lips together, looking for a moment very much like her daughter. "There are some who talk revolution, and wistfully, too. Sepik, who makes the baskets, is one. But my man comes from a line of scribes, and most of them were killed in the Pirate Wars—none of them knew aught of fighting. He's more pacifist than some."

I nodded. "I understand."

She half reached out her hand, and I took it and clasped it. With a brief curtsy she turned and disappeared back down the trail.

I wasted no time lingering but splashed down through the stream with my blue skirts held high; I toiled up the other side, crossed over the stone wall, and was on my way.

ELEVEN

I KEPT WALKING UNTIL MY ANKLE ACHED, THEN I stopped under a tree to eat. I hoped when I got to a more wooded area I might find a fallen branch that would serve as a cane. Meantime, at each of the two trickling spring streams I'd crossed, I paused long enough to drink and to soak my foot in the shocking cold water. The numbness helped.

My picnic was a quiet one, there in the shade of an old oak. I listened to birds chasing through the long grasses and distant hedgerows, and looked up at the benign blue sky. It was hard to believe right then that a great search was going on just for me.

I ate only one bread stuffed with cheese and herbs, and one fruit tart, leaving all the rest for later. I wanted the food to last as long as possible—as if the sense of peace that I'd gotten from Ara's family might disappear along with their food.

Late in the afternoon I limped my way down the last leg of the path, which joined up with a stone-paved road. My heart thumped when I saw people on the road, going both ways. I walked slowly down, relieved that none of them were warriors. Hoping this was a good sign, I fell in behind an ox-drawn cart full of early vegetables. Occasionally horses trotted up from behind. I resisted the urge to look behind me, and I made myself wait until they drew abreast. Each time it was only ordinary folk who rode by.

The traffic increased when I reached the village, and when I walked into the market square I saw a large crowd gathered at one end. For a few moments I stood uncertainly, wondering whether I ought to leave or find out what the crowd was gathered for.

Suddenly they parted, and without warning two soldiers in brown and green rode side by side straight at me. Dropping my gaze to my dusty feet, I pressed back with the rest of the people on the road near me, and listened with intense relief as their horses cantered by without pausing.

The decision as to whether I should try to find out what was going on was settled for me when the crowd around me surged forward, and a man somewhere behind me called, "Hi, there! Molk! What's toward?"

"Search," a tall, bearded man said, turning. Around me people muttered questions and comments as he added, "That Countess causing all the problems up-mountain. Milord Commander Debegri has taken over the search, and he thinks she might end up this far south."

"Reward?" a woman's shrill voice called from somewhere to the left.

"Promised sixty in pure gold."

"Where from?" someone else yelled. "If it's Debegri, I wouldn't count no gold 'less I had it in hand, and then I'd test it."

This caused a brief, loud uproar of reaction, then the bearded man bellowed, "The King! Sixty for information that proves true. Double that for a body. Preferably alive, though they don't say by how much."

Some laughed, but there was an undertone of shock from others.

Then: "What's she look like, and is she with anyone?"

"Might be on a brown mare. Filthy clothes, looks like a human rat, apparently. No hat. Dressed like a dockside beggar."

"That's some help." Another woman laughed. "I take it we look for whiskers and a long tail?"

"Short, scrawny, brown hair, long—very long. Blue eyes. Bandaged left leg, got caught in a steel trap. Probably limping if not mounted."

Limping. I looked down, wondering if any of the people pressed around me had been watching me walk.

Time to move on. Now, I thought, and I took a step sideways, then backward, easing my way out of the crowd. I didn't hear all of the next shouted question, but the answer was clear enough: "Commander Debegri said that if anyone is caught harboring or aiding the fugitive, it means death."

One step, two: I turned and walked away, forcing myself to keep an even pace, as my heart thumped like a drum right under my ears.

Of course I couldn't get away from that village fast enough.

On my way in I'd turned over various plans in my mind, mostly false tales about stolen money and a desperately ill relative, meant to get me a free bed (or a corner in a barn), for it was increasingly apparent that rain was on the way. Now I abandoned those, glad I had spoken to no one. When the rain started I clutched my basket to me and tried to hurry my pace, to look like I had somewhere to go, because it seemed to me that passersby glanced at me curiously.

As soon as I could find a side road I turned down it, and then an even smaller one than that, scarcely more than a cow path. Which brought me unexpected luck; just as the sun was setting, I spotted an outbuilding on what seemed to be a good-sized farm. A cautious scouting proved it to be empty of anyone but a number of chickens. They put up a squawk and murmur when I first walked in, but when I'd settled myself on some piled straw, they ignored me after a time.

The last of the light sufficed to enable me to get some food and repack my basket, then I arranged the straw into as comfortable a pile as I could, curled up, and fell asleep to the steady beat of rain on the metal roof.

By sunup I was on my way again. Remembering that nasty

comment about the filthy dockside beggar, I dusted myself off and straightened my bodice and skirt, then I took the added precaution of wrapping my braid around my head in a coronet, tucking the end under, then retying the kerchief. This way, I hoped, I looked as anonymous as possible.

My ankle felt much the same as it had the previous morning, which boded well enough if I were careful. I ate as I walked, resolving to try to find something to use as a cane at least for a time. My plan was to make my way steadily west, then worry about the northern trip once I was safely into the mountains. Around me now were rolling hills, some forest-covered. This made for nice cover and some protection from the intermittent rain, but unfortunately the clouds were so thick and low they thoroughly obscured the sun—and the distant mountains. I had nothing to guide myself by.

I tried to choose larger hills to traverse, figuring that this would bring me steadily west and mountainward. It was good theory but bad practice—which I didn't realize until I topped a rocky cliff and looked down at a wide river meandering its way along. It had to be the Akaeriki—there was no river this large north of Remalna-city except the Akaeriki. And there were no rivers at all running north-south.

I looked back. Tired, footsore, I did not want to simply retrace my steps. So I turned west and walked along the ridge parallel to the river, deciding that I would choose a direction if I reached civilization. Otherwise—since I was there—I'd look for an easy way to cross the river, which had to be done sometime anyway.

On the far side was the main Akaeriki road. Twice I saw the continuous stream of traffic pull aside for galloping formations of spear-carrying soldiers. The second time I saw them riding headlong toward the east, my worry was replaced by a kind of gloating triumph.

This gave me the impetus to push on, threading my way steadily through increasingly wild country. The rain had largely abated, though out on the horizon a solid black line of clouds made me determined not to stop for the night until I'd found some kind of substantial shelter.

The impending rain was on my mind when I reached an intersecting path that led down an ancient ravine to an old, narrow bridge. No one was on it. As I watched, hesitating, a white-bearded shepherd approached from the other side, clucking to a flock of sheep.

No one appeared to disturb them as they crossed. A short time later the sheep appeared on the path just below me, and I ducked behind a rock as they trotted by, followed up by their shuffling human.

One more glance—and I slipped down the trail and stepped out onto the bridge, which vibrated with each step. Avoiding looking down at the rocky river below, I hurried across, then stepped onto the north bank with a sense of relief.

I crossed the road quickly, saw only a boy driving a cart loaded with hay. Scrambling up the low ridge on the other side, I soon achieved the relative safety of a scattering of trees.

And so for a time—I heard bells echo through the valley, tolling second-green and third-green—I walked above the road where days ago I had been taken in the other direction by Shevraeth on his dapple-gray. That journey was on my mind as I toiled through grass and over stones and the thick tree roots of ancient hemlock.

The forestland thickened at one point, and without warning it opened onto a road. Fading back behind a screen of ferns, I watched the traffic. It appeared I'd reached a major crossroads. A stone marker at the intersection indicated the Akaeriki road downhill, and to the north lay the town of Thoresk.

A town. Surely one anonymous female could lose herself in a town? And while she was at it, find some shelter?

Big raindrops started plopping in the leaves around me. The coming storm wouldn't be warded by tree branches and leaves, that was for certain. Clutching my half-empty basket to my side, I started up the road, careful not to limp if anyone came into view from the opposite direction.

I saw a line of slow wagons up ahead, with a group of small children gamboling around them. I hurried my pace slightly so I would look like I belonged with them; I had nearly caught up when a deep thundering noise seemed to vibrate up from the ground.

"Cavalcade! Cavalcade!" a high childish voice shrieked.

The farmers clucked at their oxen and the wagons hulked and swung, metal frames creaking, over to one side. The children ran up the grassy bank beside the road, hopping and shrieking with excitement.

Feeling my knees go suddenly watery, I scrambled up the bank as well, then sat in the grass with my basket on my lap. I checked my kerchief surreptitiously and snatched my hand down as two banner-carrying outriders galloped into view around the bend I'd walked so shortly before.

Behind them a single rider cantered on a nervous white horse. The rider was short but strongly built. A gray beard, finicky mustache, and long hair marked him as a noble; his mouth and eyes were narrowed, whether in habit or in anger I didn't know—but my instinctive reaction to him was fear.

He wore the plumed helm of a commander, and his battle tunic was brown velvet. He had passed by before I realized that I had very nearly come face-to-face with Baron Nenthar Debegri, Galdran Merindar's former—and now present—commander.

Then behind him came row on row of soldiers, all formidably armed, riding three abreast. Dust and mud flew from the horses' hooves, and the noise was enough to set the oxen bellowing in distress and pulling at their traces. Seven, eight, nine ridings—a full wing.

A full wing of warriors, all to search for me? I didn't know whether to laugh or to faint in terror. So I just sat there numbly and watched them all ride by—a very strange kind of review.

As the end of the cavalcade at last drew nigh, the children were already skidding down the bank. My eyes, caught by a change in color, lifted. Instead of rows of brown-and-green battle gear, the last portion were in blue with black and white, their device three stars above a coronet. As my astonished mind registered that this was the Renselaeus device, my gaze was drawn to the single rider leading their formation.

A single rider on a dapple-gray. Tall in the saddle, long blond hair flying in the wind, hat so low it shadowed the upper portion of his face, the Marquis of Shevraeth rode by.

And as he drew abreast, his head lifted slightly, turned, and he stared straight into my eyes.

TWELVE

THERE WAS NO TIME TO REACT, OF COURSE.

My heart gave one great thump and scampered like the rat they'd called me as the gray rode on unchecked, followed by the remainder of the cavalcade.

Ahead of me, the oxen drivers and their children moved back slowly onto the road, the adults exclaiming and wondering what was going on, and the children whooping and waving imaginary swords.

The only thought in my mind was to put as much distance as possible between that town and myself.

Go east, I thought. *They won't expect that.*

And I turned my nose back into the forest from which I'd emerged, and started hurrying along as fast as I could.

In the meantime my mind was busy arguing with itself. I could see Shevraeth's face clearly—as if the moment had been painted against the insides of my eyelids. It was impossible to say that there had been recognition; maybe only a reminder. His expression certainly hadn't changed from what had to be a kind of resigned boredom.

And it's not like he's ever seen me with a clean face, I thought, grimacing as I remembered that bearded man's description. My hair was hidden, I was wearing a gown usually worn by prosperous farm girls, and of course I'd been sitting, so there was no limp or bandage to give me away.

Just a scare, I told myself. *He was watching the crowd to pass the time.* But my heart persisted in hammering at my ribs, and my feet sped along as though there were fire at my heels.

The rain was coming down in earnest when I dropped onto a footpath. With relief I turned and followed this, and I soon emerged from the forest into a sheltered little dell.

The welcome gold of lit windows glowed through the gathering darkness. I was in a tiny village.

They can't possibly find me here, I thought as I splashed down the path. *Probably no one but the inhabitants even knows where the village is.*

So thinking, I scouted my way around the nearest buildings, and when I found a huge barn, I didn't even hesitate to slip inside.

It had to be a common barn; there were numerous animals housed inside. But it was warm and dry, and someone had even left a lamp sitting on a hen coop just inside the door.

I looked around, saw a hayloft and a ladder. In the space of three breaths I was up it and lying down on a pile of fresh, sweet-smelling hay. Shivering from my wet clothes, I wished I dared to take them off as I rummaged in my basket for some food.

The bread had grown hard and the cheese dry, but the fruit was still tasty. I decided I had to finish the last of the bread, and save the fruit tart for the morrow. After that, I'd be on my own.

As if to taunt me, savory food smells wafted up to my rafter. I sighed—then realized that the door below must have been opened. And a moment later I rolled over toward the ladder and stared into a pair of wary green eyes.

"Awk!" I squeaked.

The eyes crinkled. The owner took another step up the ladder, and a buxom young woman around my own age, with a cloud of curling red hair, faced me. Her face was moon-round, her eyes interested. "You left wet footprints across the dirt," she said.

I sighed. "It's just the storm. I was on my way home, and it rained so very hard, and I'll go if you like."

She shrugged, smiling a little. "Truth is, I don't care a bit, but if Grandfer comes out, he'll raise a ruckus. Inn does bad enough in these times, as he reminds us every time we want a new hair ribbon or a coin to go to the fair."

"Haven't any coins. Shall I sweep the prints away?"

"I will, soon's I feed the animals." She winked. "Go ahead and sleep. I won't tell—truth is, times aplenty I've thought of running away from Grandfer, except what would I do to earn my keep anywhere else except tend farm stock? May's well do that at home, for who's to say that anyone who might hire me might not be three times worse?"

She think's I'm a runaway apprentice. "Oh, thank you!"

She shrugged again, started down, then stopped when her eyes were once more level with the edge of the rafter. They crinkled as she said, "I just wish you'd been a boy instead, and as handsome, for then I'd have demanded a kiss as payment."

And with a gurgling laugh, she descended the rest of the way.

I chewed at my tough bread and listened to the rain on the roof and the pleasant sounds of the animals getting their food. Presently I heard the rhythmic *wisp*ing of a broom, and then the door closed.

And it seemed I'd just shut my eyes and drifted off to sleep when light flickered into my dreams and I opened my eyes on the red-haired girl, clutching a candle whose flame flickered wildly. Her face was white with excitement and fear.

"Are you a countess?" she whispered.

A pang smote my chest, and I sat up. "Who is out there?"

She pointed behind her. "Warriors. A whole riding, at least. And a lord. Rings, a sword—" She gestured, obviously impressed, then the fear was back. "Going from house to house. I told Grandfer I was checking on the cow about to calve," she added from down on the barn floor. "If they find out you're here—"

"I'll go."

She was gone in a trice, leaving me to feel my way down in the darkness. *Leastwise if I can't see, no one can see me—unless they have a torch, and then I'll see their light first,* I thought.

The barn had several doors. I eased one open a crack as somewhere nearby a horse shifted weight and nickered softly. Terrified that the sound would carry, I slipped out the door and shut it.

Rain hit me in the face, hard and cold. I stumbled out into it, my feet splashing in deep puddles. Running as fast as I could, I crossed behind another building and then nearly hit a tree. Its ferny leaves warned me to stop. I reached, felt the bole of a mighty hemlock, and after only a short hesitation, I tucked my basket securely up under my arm and climbed the tree as high as I could.

Shivering, my fingers and toes numb, I stared down through the branches until I saw lights flickering, and over the steady drumming of the rain I heard horses' hooves. The streaming torches bounced away up a trail and disappeared.

I clung to the tree until my arms were so numb I couldn't tell if I was holding on or not. This made me panicky again; and shakily, moving with excruciating slowness, I climbed back down.

On the muddy ground I hesitated, wishing I dared to retreat to the barn again. But I remembered that business about "harboring the fugitive" and "death," and reluctantly I felt my way farther back into the forest, until the growth around me was so tangled the rain was a mere nuisance instead of a downpour.

Worming my way into the thickest part of a patch of ferns, I curled up and passed the remainder of a miserable night. Sleep was intermittent, for sudden drips of cold on my skin, or the tickle of some unseen insect, would keep jerking me awake. The night seemed endless, but at last a bleak, cheerless blue light lifted the shadows just enough for me to make out the shapes of branches and foliage. By then I had wound myself into a tight ball, and what little warmth I could generate made me ill inclined to move.

But I knew I had to move eventually, if only to better shelter. My joints ached, my foot itched, and I was afraid that once again I might get sick, and this time there would be no Ara and her nice family to rescue me.

Still I stayed where I was until the light was stronger, and then shafts of yellow stabbed into my hidey-hole. I realized that the sun had come out. Hoping for warmth, I moved, this time with alacrity, and soon I was making my way westward into the forest, moving from sun patch to sun patch.

By noon I had dried out. I stopped once and beat as much of the dirt off as I could, which rendered my clothing a little less stiff. When I came to a stream I washed my face and hands. Whatever happened, I did not want to look like that filthy dockside beggar they were noising about over half the countryside.

On my walk I ate the last of my food, and when I found another stream, I drank enough to fill my middle.

Now I had an additional worry: finding food. And as the day wore on, it became increasingly obvious that this was going to be as hard as staying out of sight of searchers.

When I reached the end of the patch of forest I was ready to run out into the bright sunshine—but before I'd passed the last tree I saw a line of riders racing across a distant field.

Ducking instinctively behind the tree, I peered over a branch, shading my eyes against the glare of the sun, and saw that they rode in two-by-two formation, and that they were not following any road.

Now, it *might* have been the riders had nothing to do with me, but I was not about to take that chance. As I looked out across the rolling terrain, I realized that they probably had me boxed in. They knew approximately where I was—that business the night before made it pretty clear—but not exactly. As for my part, I had to spot their perimeter . . . and cross it.

And get something to eat.

Without endangering any innocent people.

Standing there watching the diminishing formation, I was intensely aware of how alone I was—but it was not the same terrible, helpless feeling I'd had when I first discovered that I was a prisoner. Then I couldn't walk and couldn't get free. Now I was free, and I could walk, and as I remembered what Ara had said about that accursed Shevraeth and his abominable friend making sport of finding me, I got angry. There is nothing like good, honest, righteous anger to infuse a person with energy.

All right, I thought. *Either I keep blundering about in all four directions, or else I locate these searchers—they have to be a limited number—and then move when and where they are least expecting it.*

And so I turned my steps west and started stumping along in the direction the cross-country racers had gone.

I crossed two hills, cresting the last to look down into a pleasant little valley. Water ribboned between the hills from a small lake, probably going to join up with the Akaeriki south of me. Along the lakeside lay a small town. There was no sign of my search party anywhere around; they were probably in the town. So I found a good spot in the shelter of a thick shrub—for by then the sun was hot—made certain that no part of me formed a silhouette, and sat down to watch.

I was fighting drowsiness when they finally emerged and started riding southward, again across the hills. I stared after them until my eyes watered. They kept disappearing beyond the hills but then eventually reappeared, each time getting smaller and smaller. Then they disappeared for a long time: another village or town. I made myself wait and watch. Again I was trying not to nod off when I saw a second line appear on the crest of a hill directly west of me, on the other lip of the valley.

The urge to sleep fled. I watched the line—it was a long one this time, with tiny bright dots at the front that indicated banners —descend into the town.

The banners meant the commander. Was the Marquis still with him, or had he finally gotten bored and gone back to the silk-and-velvet life in Athanarel?

"You might contemplate the purpose of a court..." You brainless, *twaddling idiot*, I thought scornfully. I wished he were before me. I wished I could personally flout him and his busy searchers, and make him look like the fool he was. And watch the reaction, and walk away laughing.

While I was indulging my fulminating imaginings, the long line emerged again, much more quickly than the previous one had. Delight suffused me: They had obviously discovered that the previous group had been there, and had probably decided that the place was therefore safe.

Excellent. Then that was where I would go.

The sun was setting and a cold wind had started fretting at the tops of the grass, fingering my skirts and kerchief, when I topped the last rise on my approach to the lakeside town. Keeping well to the undergrowth, I skirted the place, looking for a likely hidey-hole, preferably one in which I might also find something to eat. Barns seemed the best choice. I had only to sneak in when the owners were safely abed. And maybe there'd be some early vegetables or even some preserves, if I were really lucky.

I waited until dark had fallen and then started slinking my way down along someone's garden wall. Dropping onto a brick pathway, I straightened up with my basket on my arm and tried to look unconcerned. People were walking about, and the ironwork lamps on poles lighting the streets indicated this was customary. Obviously this wasn't a market town that closed its doors at sundown. Perhaps it was one of those towns where wealthy merchants bought a second house in pleasant surroundings for purely social purposes. Certainly a lakeside would be pleasant enough.

As I emerged onto a lovely brick-patterned street some of the noise I heard resolved into music. My steps turned automatically that way, and I saw an inn, its windows bright with golden light, its doors wide open. As always when I heard music, my heart felt light and the tiredness in my body diminished. This was good music, too, not just the awkward plunkings and tweetings that served merely to mark the right melody for enthusiastic but untrained singers, as I was used to in Tlanth. It had been a very long while since a minstrel, much less wandering players, had dared our mountain heights. Though we did love entertainment, the word had probably spread down-mountain that about all they'd get from us for their pains would be loud applause and a bit of plain food.

But this inn seemed to have no such problem. Stepping inside, I counted six different instruments, all of them played well. The noises of people having a good time made listening difficult, so I pressed between merrymakers, trying to get closer to the musicians.

Someone moved, someone else changed position, and I found myself wedged against a table against one wall—a high table with ironwork chairs, instead of the usual low tables and cushions. The metal frame of the table dug into my hip, but at least no one could push me away, and I had a reasonably good view of the musicians.

And so I stood for a time, swaying and nodding with the complicated rhythms. People got up and danced, something I longed to do. I told myself it was just as well that I did not know any of the latest steps, for the last thing I needed was to risk drawing attention to myself—especially if my ankle suddenly twinged and gave out.

It did ache, I realized as I stood there, and my stomach growled and rumbled. But it was so good to be warm, and to feel safe, and to listen to—

A player faltered; the musicians stopped. Around me the voices altered a little, from loud and jovial to questioning. I felt tension dart through the room, like a frightened bird. Faces turned toward the door. Terror leaped in me as I shifted my shoulder just a little, then peeked swiftly under the gesturing arm of the man standing next to me.

Baron Debegri stood at the entrance. He negligently waved a gloved hand toward the table he wanted—a central table, with the best view of the musicians. Two stone-faced warriors motioned to the people already seated there.

No word had been spoken. The people at the table picked up their dishes and glasses and disappeared silently into the crowd. Debegri sat down, hands on thighs, looking well pleased with himself.

I stared at him, astounded at my amazingly bad luck. But of course he wouldn't search at night. And of course he'd quarter himself in the best place available, and if this were indeed a resort town, the inns would be the best.

I couldn't stop sneaking peeks at him as he was served a substantial meal and a bottle of what had to be the very best bluewine. No one sat with him, but one of his personal guards stood at the doorway, another behind his chair, silent, watchful, awaiting his command. He didn't offer them anything to eat, just sat there and gorged himself.

As I watched, my fear slowly turned into anger, and then to rage. Heady with hunger, I struggled within myself. I felt if I didn't do something, make some kind of gesture, I would be a coward forever.

The rich smell of wine-braised onions met my nose, making me swallow. I turned, saw a harassed waiter laying down a bowl of some kind of stew for the people whose table I was wedged against. A flagon of mead and plate of fresh-sliced kresp were next. I met the eyes of the man seated adjacent. He met my gaze incuriously, then looked away with an air of slight annoyance. The other man paid me not the slightest heed as he piled kresp onto his plate and then ladled savory-smelling fish stew over it.

"*Ungh,*" I groaned. Luckily the sound was lost in the voices, which had risen again.

The music started up, this time a merry rhythm that made some people start clapping in counterpoint. Dancers appeared, at first staying well away from Debegri's table. However, after four or five songs, the crowd was thicker than ever, and slowly, surely, the dancers moved closer, until the flash of embroidered sleeves and the whirl of skirts flickered between me and the King's commander. For a time my attention was divided between sneaking glimpses at the two men beside me, who never once looked up from their meal before it was all gone, and the Baron, whose table was loaded with goodies, some of which he didn't even touch.

And as I watched the dancers moving unheeded around him, an idea formed in my mind, a reckless, useless, stupid idea, but one that promised such fun I could almost hear Bran's laughter.

It's been too long since I heard him laugh, I realized grimly. I was gloriously angry at the whole world—at the commander sitting there at his ease, at his numerous soldiery all looking for my dockside-rat self, at the Marquis for scorning us and our ideals, at the ordinary people for not caring that Bran had worn himself tired and grim on their behalf when he should have been laughing and moving right along with all these dancers.

The dancers had been a brightly colored mass, but now I watched individuals. One in particular drew my eye: a big bull of a man, obviously half-drunk. His partner could hardly stop laughing when he lurched and staggered as the others twirled and stamped. I watched the figures of the dance, learning the pattern. The observers seemed to know it well, for when the stomping and clapping occurred, those who wished to cross the room threaded their way among the dancers; then when the couples did hands-high, the floor cleared for the resulting whirls and partner trades.

The drunk man was starting to look tired. He'd want to stop soon, I knew. I'd have to move now, or not at all.

My heart clumped in counterpoint to the music as I slipped

through the crowd around the perimeter of the room and then, just as the clap-stamp-clap-stamp commenced, eased my way out among the dancers, ducking a tray here and a swinging arm there. My basket handle was over my elbow, so both hands were free.

When the horns signaled the next hands-high, I remembered my lessons from Khesot on Using Your Opponent's Weight Against Him. Steadying my hand against the drunken man's shoulder, I hooked my good foot around his ankle and yanked, pushing his shoulder at the same time.

He spun, bellowing, his fingers clutching at air, and fell—right across the commander's table. His partner shrieked, waving her arms. I dodged between her and Debegri, who had leaped up, cursing, as he mopped at the wine splashed down his front. With one hand I nipped a chicken pie and with the other a cup of mulled dessert wine, just before the table crashed over on its side, flinging the food everywhere. People screamed and shouted, pushing and shoving to get away from the mess. I ducked between two dancers and backed, laughing breathlessly, toward the door.

The drunken man was yelling, "Where is she? Where is she? Where's the little snipe that tripped me?"

"Calm yourself, sir," Debegri grated, his voice harsh and somehow familiar. "Guards! Right this table . . ."

Trying to smother my laughter, I turned around on the doorstep and saw another chance. A single warrior stood holding the reins of the beautiful white horse. As I watched, the soldier stifled a yawn and looked over at the door, to where the two guards were busy with Debegri's table.

Flinging the mulled wine squarely into her face, I jumped up across the horse's back, and as it bucked and sidled, I jammed my heels in its ribs and it leaped forward.

The reins went flying. I grabbed at them with my free hand and thrust the meat pie into my mouth with the other.

The warrior sprang to stop me but the horse was too fast. I dashed my basket against the warrior's head and slapped the reins on the horse's white neck.

A spear whizzed right past my shoulder, and a few moments later something sharp pricked my neck. Ducking as low as I could, I clung desperately to the reins. The horse stretched its legs into a gallop, and then a canter. Behind I heard the blare of a summons horn.

The chase was on!

THIRTEEN

I KNEW IT HAD BEEN A STUPID THING TO DO—AND
worse, dangerous. But I simply could not stop laughing. Half of my
meat pie fell away in my struggle to get and keep my balance. What
little I did manage to hang on to tasted wonderful—and woke up
my appetite like some kind of ravening beast.

I stayed low, for the white horse was astonishingly fast and I
was afraid to fall. I was also afraid of spears, or worse; remembering
the sharp prick at my neck, I touched my skin cautiously and found
the slime of blood and a long rent in my kerchief. That warrior
had recovered pretty fast from the mulled wine in the face. If her
aim had been just a fraction better, Debegri would have had a head
all ready for the King's gatepost.

But for now the worry lessened slightly; my horse was faster
than the pursuers'. The problem was I had no idea where I was
going. Every curve frightened me, even though my mount pulled
steadily ahead. I kept scanning the hilltops fearfully, expecting a
contingent to top the rise and cut me off.

Despite my lengthening lead—and maybe because of it—the
pursuers stayed hot to task.

Finally I thought of the forest and looked around again, this
time to get my bearings. As soon as we rounded a likely curve in

the stone road I yanked the reins to the side. The horse leaped to obey, and with a heave and a snort started plunging crosswise up the hill to the east.

I didn't really think this would fool the pursuers, and sure enough, after a short time I saw their outlines against the uneasy dark of the sky. And moments after that, a cold sweep of wind brought the first spattering of another rainstorm.

It would slow me, but so would it slow the others. The forest line neared . . . neared . . . much faster to reach now than it had been to leave by foot. I realized as my mount flashed past the first trees that I'd make it—but what then? Try to lose them? That tactic wouldn't last long, not with a great white horse crashing and smashing through the undergrowth.

And . . . for the first time I thought of the handsome saddle equipage on the animal's back. What if Debegri had one of those summons-stones? All they'd have to do was follow along and pounce when it was convenient.

Yet if I somehow managed to ditch the horse in the forest and it emerged without me, they'd have a most conveniently narrow perimeter in which to search.

But if they thought I was still on its back . . .

The trees were closer together. Unseen branches whipped at my face and head. I let the animal slow just a little as I fumbled the basket off my arm and hooked the handle over the pommel. How to keep it there? I thought of the kerchief. With a pang of regret I pulled it off. I wouldn't be able to wear it anymore anyway, not with that great rent in it, and no doubt splashes of gore from where the warrior's knife had nicked my skin.

Tying one end around the basket handle and the pommel, I let the other end flap in the breeze. Would that fool them into thinking I was still on the horse? I'd have to try.

The rain was now coming down in earnest, roaring through the trees. I could not see or hear the pursuit, but that meant nothing. Slowing the white horse as much as I dared, I pulled my legs up, readying. Ahead I saw open space, and I realized I'd have to make my move immediately.

So I guided the horse to a tree with a nice low branch, stood on the saddle...reached...gripped rough bark...and with my right foot gave the horse's flank a good smack. "Run!" I yelled, scrambling up onto the branch.

My braid came loose, its coils catching round my neck and nearly strangling me, but I ignored it as I fought my way up into the tree and then held on tightly. The wet, slick branches swayed with the wind, and rain stung my face.

I scarcely had time to get a good grip. A frighteningly short interval passed before I heard crashing noises above the roar of rain, and through the tossing branches saw a weird reddish glow bobbing crazily below. The pursuit passed right below me, following the trail of smashed grass and small bushes that the white horse had made.

If I'd been just a little slower, they would have seen me.

Instinct was strong. I wanted to hug that tree tight and stay there for the duration, but I knew this would be a mistake. I had to get out of that forest, and fast, for I couldn't count on my basket decoy lasting too long.

So, slipping and grunting, I climbed down and then stumbled back along the trail the plunging horses had made.

It wound around a bit, certainly more than I had been aware of when on horseback. Trying to decide whether this was bad or good, I toiled on, gasping for breath and looking frequently behind me.

When I emerged from the forest, I wondered, *What now?*

The town. Why not? They will never expect me there again.

And so, as exhaustion slowed my steps, I made my way for the second time back to the town, stopping only once, to drink from a cold, fresh-running stream.

I kept well away from the inn. The streets were mostly clear. Occasional pairs of warriors clopped by on horseback, bearing torches and spears. By then I was too tired to react much beyond ducking into the shadows.

I found a garden with little open-air gazebos placed at intervals along a path, and a very pretty bathhouse on a stream. These were a temptation, but I avoided them. They'd be the first thing *I* would check if I were searching.

So, once again, I found a thick ferny plant to crawl under, and there I passed the night.

Despite my discomfort I slept heavily, but I woke feeling like I needed a goodly week more of sleep. My face, hands, and legs below my knees hurt as though they'd been stung by a thousand nettles, and when I looked, I saw my skin crisscrossed by red welts from the branches and twigs the night before.

My ankle throbbed warningly. Two of the healing scabs had been ripped off and the whole thing was fairly messy again—though of course not as bad as it had been at first. Just once I looked at the bathhouse, from which I could hear congenial voices echoing, and I yearned for a bath. How long had it been, aside from the one day at Ara's? *Never again will I complain about our old bathhouse*, I thought grimly as I flexed my foot. I knew I wasn't going to be walking any great distances that day. So what I had to do was to find a way to get a ride.

Of course the first thing I thought of was all those wagons I'd seen on my peregrinations. But I was certain there were warriors stopping every cart that came along any of the main roads. And the little side paths were too narrow for wagons.

Just then the bells for first-gold rang. Dawn. The fewer people who saw me the better, I thought, looking down at the once-pretty blue skirt. Now it was splotched with mud and striped with grass and leaf stains.

I thrust my braid down the back of my underdress to hide its length, smoothed my bodice and skirt as best as I could, and made certain no one was around before I crawled out from beneath my fern.

It seemed strange not to have the basket on my arm. I missed its comforting weight, even though it would have served no further use.

I miss Ara's clean bed, and her pretty garden, and that hot food...

I shook my head, ignoring the pangs through my temples. No use in regrets—I had to keep my spirits up.

I crossed the garden, staying near the hedgerow borders until the pathway debouched onto one of the lovely brick streets. A quick glance down the street revealed scarcely any traffic—but way up at the other end were two tall, armed individuals wearing blue and black-and-white livery.

Which meant the Marquis was somewhere around.

For a moment I indulged in a brief but satisfying daydream of scoring off him as I had off the Baron the night before. But amusing as the daydream was, I was *not* about to go searching him out.

First of all, while I didn't look like I had before, the dress wasn't much of a disguise; and second...I frowned. Despite his reputation as a fop and a gamester, I wasn't all that certain he would react as slowly as Debegri had.

I retreated back to the garden to think out my next step. Mist was falling, boding ill weather for the remainder of the day. And my stomach felt as if it had been permanently pressed against the back of my spine.

I pulled the laces of the bodice tighter, hoping that would help, then sat on a rock and propped my elbows on my knees.

"Are you lost?"

The voice, a quiet one, made me start violently. My shoulders came up defensively as I turned to face an elderly man. He was elegantly dressed, wearing a fine hat in the latest fashion, and carried no weapons.

"Oh no. I was supposed to meet someone here, and..." I shrugged, thinking wildly. "A—a flirt," I added, I don't know why. "I guess he changed his mind." I got to my feet again.

The man smiled a little. "It happens more frequently than not when one is young, if you'll forgive my saying so."

"Oh, I know." I waved my hands as I backed up one step, then another. "They smile, and dance, and then go off with someone else. But I'll just find someone better. So I'll be on my way," I babbled.

He nodded politely, almost a bow, and I whirled around and scurried down the path.

Even more intensely than before, I felt that crawling sensation down my spine, so I dropped off the path and circled back. I was slightly reassured when I saw the old man making his way slowly along the path as though nothing out of the ordinary had happened; but my relief was very short lived.

As I watched, two equerries in Renselaeus livery strode along the path, overtook the man, and addressed him. I watched with my heart thumping like a drum as the man spoke at some length, brushed his fingers against his face—*the scratches from the trees!*— and then gestured in the direction I had gone.

Expecting the two equerries to immediately take off after me, I braced for a run. *Why had I babbled so much?* I thought, annoyed with myself. *Why didn't I just say "No" and leave?*

But the equerries both turned and walked swiftly back in the direction they'd come, and the old man continued on his way.

What does that mean?

And the answer was not long in coming: They were going back to report.

Which meant a whole lot of them searching. And soon.

Yes, I'd really widened my perimeter, I thought furiously, cursing the Baron, music, inns, resorts, food, and the Baron again, throwing in Galdran Merindar *and* the Marquis of Shevraeth for good measure. I slipped back through the garden to the street. Spotting an alley behind a row of houses, I ducked into that.

And when I heard the thunder of approaching horses' hooves, I dove toward the first door, which was miraculously open. Slipping inside, a sickly smile on my face, I concocted a wild story about deliveries and the wrong address as I looked about for inhabitants angered at my intrusion.

But my luck had turned a little: The hallway was empty. Behind me was a stairway leading upward, and next to it one leading to a basement. For a moment I wanted to fling myself down that, to hide in the dark, but I restrained myself: There was generally only one way out of a basement.

At my right a plain door-tapestry opened onto a storeroom of some sort. I peeked inside. There were two windows with clouded glass, and a jumble of dishes, small pieces of furniture, trays, and a row of hooks with aprons and caps on them. That outer door was the servants' entrance, I realized, and this room was their store-room.

Colors flickering in the clouded glass brought my attention around. Moving right up next to the window, I listened, and heard the slow clopping of hooves. The rhythm broke, then stopped; from another direction came more hooves, which swiftly got closer.

The house I was in was a corner house, the first in a row. Two search parties met right outside my window, where the alley conjoined with the street.

"Nothing this way, my lord," someone said.

A horse sidled; another whickered.

Then a familiar voice said, not ten paces from me: "Search the houses."

FOURTEEN

So there i was, light-headed with hunger, foot-sore, with the perimeter of safety having closed to about ten paces around me, and the Marquis of Shevraeth standing just on the other side of the wall.

At least he didn't—yet—know it.

As if in answer, I heard the *klunk* of footsteps on the tiled floor directly above me. Someone else had been listening at a window and was now moving about. To come downstairs? Would the searchers go to the front or come to the back?

I thought about, then dismissed, the idea of begging safety from the inhabitants. If they were not mercifully inclined, all they'd need to do was shout for help and I'd be collared in a wink. And if they *were* merciful, they faced a death sentence if caught hiding me.

No, what I had to do was get out without *anyone* knowing I'd been inside the house. And nippily, too.

Hearing the clatter of hooves and the jingle of harnesses and weapons, I edged close to the window and peered out again. All I could see was the movement of smeary colors, but it sounded like one riding had moved on. To divide up and start on the houses?

What about the other group?

Dark-hued stalks stood directly outside the window. Did one of them have a pale yellow top?

I could just *see* him standing there narrow eyed, looking around. Then maybe he'd glance at the window and see something flesh-colored and blue just inside the edge...

I closed my eyes, feeling a weird vertigo. Of course he couldn't see me—it was dark inside and light out. That meant the window would be a blank, dark square to him. If he even gave it a look. I was letting fancy override my good sense, and if I didn't stop it, his searchers would find me standing there daydreaming.

I took a deep breath—and the stalks outside the window began to move. Soon they were gone from sight, and nothing changed in the window at all. I heard no more feet or hooves or swords clanking in scabbards.

It was time for me to go.

My heart thumped in time to the pang in my temples as I opened the storeroom door, peeked out, then eased the outside door open. Nothing... nothing... I slipped out into the alley.

And saw two posted guards at the other end. They were at that moment looking the other way. I whisked myself behind a flowering shrub that bordered the street, wincing as I waited for the yells of "Stop! You!"

Nothing.

Breathing hard, I ran full speed back across the street and into the garden where I'd spent the night before. And with no better plan in mind, I sped along the paths to the shady section, found my fern, and crawled back in. The soil was still muddy and cold, but I didn't mind; I curled up, closed my eyes, and tried to calm my panicking heart and aching head.

And slept.

And woke to the marching of feet and jingling of weaponry. Before I could move, there was a crackling of foliage and a spear-head thrust its way into my bush, scarcely an arm's length above my head. It was withdrawn, the steps moved on, and I heard the smashing sound of another poke into the shrubbery there.

"This is my third time through here," a low voice muttered.

"I tell you, if we don't get a week's leave when this is over, I'm going back to masonry. Just as much work, but at least you get enough time to sleep," another voice returned.

There was a snorting laugh, then the footsteps moved on.

I lay in frightened relief, wondering what to do next. My tongue was sticky in my mouth, for I'd had nothing to drink since the night before, and of course nothing to eat but those few bites of the meat pie.

How much longer can I do this?

Until I get home, I told myself firmly.

I'd wait until dark, sneak out of that town, and never return. *I'll travel by night and go straight west,* I decided. How I was to get food I didn't know, but I was already so light-headed from hunger, all I could think of was getting away.

Just before sunset it started to rain again. I told myself that this was good, that it limited visibility for the searchers. Therefore it would help me, because I needed to go west, and I'd been trapped on the east side of the town for two days.

Thus I rationalized sneaking through the town rather than going around it, which might be a small problem to those on horseback—but to someone who was tired, footsore, and unenthusiastic about slogging knee-deep in mud when she could traverse more quickly the beautifully paved streets, it was a lure that could not be overcome.

So, keeping to dark alleys and tree-shaded parkways, I started to make my way through the town, always edging north, since I remembered that the lake lay along the south-west border. I was doing all right until my growing thirst got so bad I could think of little else.

Where to get a drink? In the countryside this was less of a problem, but now I began to regret having stayed in the town just to make it easier on my feet. The streams had been turned into canals, with windowed bathhouses everywhere along them, and house windows overlooking everything else. It was impossible to sneak to a canal for a drink and not be seen. Holding my mouth open to catch raindrops on my tongue only made my thirst more intense.

So when I stumbled onto a little circular park with a fountain in its center, I simply couldn't resist. A quick glance showed the square to be completely deserted. In fact, so far I hadn't seen any people at all, but I didn't consider that, beyond my brief gratitude that the rain had kept them all inside.

I hopped over a little flower border. The blooms—ghostly white in the soft glow from the lamps around the park's circumference—ran up the brick walkway and gripped the stone lip of the fountain. I opened my mouth, leaned in, and took a deep gulp.

And heard hooves. Boots.

"You, there, girl! Halt!"

Who in the *universe* ever halts when the enemy tells them to?

Of course I took off in the opposite direction, as fast as I could: running across grass, leaping neatly tended flowers. But the park was a circle, which made it easy for the riders to gallop around both ways and cut me off. I stopped, looked back. No retreat.

Meanwhile another group came running across the lawns, swords drawn. I backed up a step, two; looked this way and that; tried to break for it in the largest space, which of course was instantly closed.

There must have been a dozen of them ringing me, all with rapiers and heavier weapons gleaming gold tipped in the light from the iron-posted glowglobes and the windows of the houses.

"Report," someone barked; and then to me, "Who are you? Don't you know there is a sunset curfew?"

"Ah, I didn't know." I smoothed my skirts nervously. "Been sick. No one mentioned it..."

"Who are you?" came the question again.

"I just wanted a drink. I was sick, I think I mentioned, and didn't get any water..."

"Who are you." This time it wasn't even a question.

The game was up, of course, but who said I had to surrender meekly? "Just call me Ranisia." I named my mother, using my hardest voice. "I'm a ghost, one of Galdran Merindar's many victims."

Noises from behind caused the ring to tighten, the weapons all pointing a finger's breadth from my throat. My empty hands were at my sides, but these folks were taking no chances. Maybe they thought I *was* a ghost.

No one spoke, or moved, until the sound of heels striking the brick path made the soldiers withdraw silently.

Baron Debegri strode up, his rain cape billowing. Under his foppish mustache his teeth gleamed in a very cruel grin. He stopped within a pace of me, and with no warning whatever, backhanded me right across the face. I went flying backward, landing flat in a flower bed. The Baron stepped onto my left knee and motioned a torch bearer over. He stared down at the half-healed marks on my ankle and laughed, then jerked his thumb in a gesture of command. Two soldiers sprang to either side of me, each grabbing an arm and pulling me to my feet.

"What have you to say now, my little hero?" the Baron gloated.

"That you are a fool, the son of a fool, and the servant of the biggest—"

He swung at me again, and I tried to duck, but he grabbed me by the hair and then hit me. The world seemed to explode in stars—for a long time all I could do was gasp for breath and fight against dizziness.

When I came out of it, someone was binding my hands; then two more someones grabbed my arms again, and I was half carried back to the street. My vision was blurry. I realized hazily that a gem on his embroidered gloves must have cut my forehead, for a warm trickle ran nastily down the side of my face, which throbbed even worse than my ankle.

131

I got thrown over the back of a horse, my hands and feet bound to stirrups. From somewhere I heard Debegri's harsh voice: "Lift the curfew, but tell those smug-faced Elders that if anyone harbored this criminal, the death penalty still holds. You. Tell his lordship the Marquis that his aid is no longer necessary, and he can return to Remalna-city, or wherever he wants."

Quick footsteps ran off, and then the Baron said, "Now, to Chovilun. And don't dawdle."

Chovilun...

One of the four Merindar fortresses.

I closed my eyes.

I do not like to remember that trip.

Not that I was awake for much of it—for which I am grateful. I kept sliding in and out of consciousness, and believe me, the *out*s were more welcome than the *in*s.

I knew that Chovilun Fortress lay at the base of the mountains on the Akaeriki River, which bisects the kingdom, but I didn't know how long it took to reach it.

All I can report is that I felt pretty sick, nearly as sick as I'd been when I fell into Ara's chickenyard. Sick at heart as well, for I knew there was no escape for Meliara Astiar after all; therefore I resolved that my last job was to summon enough presence of mind to die well.

Not, of course, that the truth would ever get to Branaric. The Merindars had captured and held a kingdom by a winning combination of treachery, bullying, and lying. I had made the Baron look silly during that episode at the inn, and I knew he was going to take his revenge on me in the privacy of his fortress, making it last as long as possible. And every weakness he could get me to display was going to get noised as excruciatingly as possible over the entire kingdom—especially aimed at Tlanth.

So my only hope, therefore, was to make him so angry he'd kill me outright and save us both a lot of effort.

These were my cheery thoughts—not that my head was any too clear—as we clattered into a stone courtyard at last. The everpresent rain had nearly drowned me. My hands and feet were numb. When the guards cut me loose I fell like an old bundle of laundry onto the stone courtyard, and once again hands gripped my upper arms and yanked me upright.

This time I made no pretense of walking as I was borne into a dank tunnel, then down steep steps into an even danker, nastysmelling chamber.

And what I saw around me was a real, true-to-nightmare dungeon. Shackles, iron baskets, various prods and knives and whips and other instruments whose purpose I didn't know—and didn't want to know—were displayed on the walls around two great stained and scored tables.

A huge, ugly man in a bespattered blackweave apron motioned for the soldiers to put me into a chair with irons at arms and feet. As they did, he said, "What am I supposed to be finding out?"

Behind, the Baron said harshly, "I want to shed these wet clothes. Don't touch her until I return. This is going to last a long, long time." His gloating laugh echoed down a stone passageway.

The huge man pursed his lips, shrugged, then turned to his fire, selecting various pincers and brands to lay on a grate in the flames.

Then he came back, lifted one bushy brow at the soldiers still flanking me, and said in a low voice, "Kinda little and scrawny, this one, ain't she? What she done?"

"Countess of Tlanth," one said in a flat voice.

The man whistled, then grinned. He had several teeth missing. Then he bent closer, peered at me, and shook his head. "Looks to me like she's half done for already. Grudge or no grudge, she won't last past midnight." He grinned again, motioning to the nearest warrior. "Go ahead and put the irons on. Shall we just have a little fun while we're waiting?"

He pulled one of his brands out of the fire and stepped toward me, raising it. The sharp smell of red-hot metal made me

133

sneeze—and when I looked up, the man's mouth was open with surprise.

My gaze dropped to the knife embedded squarely in his chest, which seemed to have sprouted there. *But knives don't sprout, even in dungeons*, I thought hazily, as the torturer fell heavily at my feet. I turned my head, half rising from the chair—

And saw the Marquis of Shevraeth standing framed in the doorway. At his back were four of his liveried equerries, with swords drawn and ready.

The Marquis strolled forward, indicated the knife with a neatly gloved hand, and gave me a faint smile. "I trust the timing was more or less advantageous?"

"More or less," I managed to say before the rushing in my ears washed over me, and I passed out cold right on top of the late torturer.

FIFTEEN

Awareness came back slowly, and not very pleasantly. First were all the aches and twinges, then the dizziness, and last the sensation of movement. Before I even opened my eyes I realized that once again I was on a horse, clasped upright by an arm.

The Marquis again? Memories came flooding back—the dungeon, the Baron's horrible promise, then the knife and Shevraeth's comment about timing. The Marquis had saved me, with about the closest timing in history, from a thoroughly nasty fate. Relief was my foremost emotion, then gratitude, and then a residual embarrassment that I didn't understand and instantly dismissed. He had saved my life, and I owed him my thanks.

I opened my eyes, squinting against bright sunlight, and turned my head, words forming only to vanish when I looked up into an unfamiliar face. I closed my eyes again, completely confused. Had I dreamed it all, then? Except—where was I, and with whom?

The horse stopped, and the stranger murmured, "Drink."

Something wet touched my lips. I swallowed, then gasped as liquid fire ignited its way down my gullet, the harsh taste of distilled bristic with other herbs. I swallowed again, and my entire body glowed—even the aches diminished.

"Not too much," someone else warned.

The liquid went away. I opened my eyes again and this time saw three or four unfamiliar faces looking at me with expressions ranging from interest to concern.

I twisted my head to look into the face of the young woman holding me. She was tall and strong, with black hair worn in a coronet around her head under a plain helm. She held out a flask to someone else, who took it, capped it, dropped it into a saddlebag.

The peachy light of early morning touched the faces around me. All of them were unfamiliar. There was no sign of the Marquis of Shevraeth—or of Baron Debegri, either. I blinked, sat up straighter, then grimaced against a renewal of all my aches.

"Am I holding too tight, Lady Meliara?" the woman asked.

"I'm all right," I said a little hoarsely.

"I don't think you can ride alone quite yet."

"Sure, I can," I replied instantly.

To my surprise they all laughed—but it wasn't unkind laughter, like Baron Debegri's, or heartless laughter, like that of Galdran's Court in the throne room at Athanarel.

"We'll see, my lady," was all she said. And lifting her head: "Let's move."

Suddenly businesslike, the others ranged themselves around us in a protective formation, and the horses started forth at a steady canter.

The glow from the bristic faded, leaving me with the lassitude of someone who feels truly awful.

After a time the riders slowed, then stopped, and the woman holding me said, "Here's a good spot. Flerac, you and Jamni see to the mounts. Loris, and you three, set us up a perimeter. Amol, the Fire Stick and the stores. My lady, you and I are going down to that pool over there."

So saying, she dismounted, then lifted me down. She paused, rummaged in her saddlebag, pulled out a bundle, then said, "I am Yora Nessaren, captain of this riding. Please come this way, my lady." And she even bowed, then held out her arm for my support. I took it gratefully.

This was certainly a new twist on the various treatments I'd received. I was even more surprised when we topped a little rise shaded by trees, and looked down at a clear pool. One end was shaded, the other golden and glittering in the sun.

"First order of the day," she said with a grin, "you are to have a bath and new gear." She opened a small, carved box. A scent of summer herbs rose from it. She dug two fingers in, then slapped something gritty onto my palm. "There's some of my sandsoap." Then, putting the box away, she reached again into her bag and pulled out a new teeth cleaner. "I always carry an extra in the field."

"Thanks," I said gratefully, thinking, as I stepped down to the pool, of all those days I'd had to use the edge of my increasingly dirty underdress.

I found a flat rock on which to put my waiting soap and teeth cleaner. Moments later I flung off the last of my dirt-stiff clothes and dived into the pool. The water was clear and cold, instantly soothing the stings got from hiding in scratchy shrubs, and the rope burns on my wrists and ankles from my journey as a saddle pack to Debegri's fortress. After a good scrub from head to toe, I reached for my clothes in order to wash them out. Yora Nessaren, who'd sat on the rise staring up at the trees, turned, then shook her head. "We'll burn those old clothes, my lady—they're ruined." And she pointed to where she'd laid out a long, heavy cotton shirt, and one of the blue and black-and-white tunics, and a pair of leggings. Renselaeus's colors.

"I don't mind putting that dress back on, dirty or not," I said. "I'm used to dirt."

She gave me a friendly shrug but shook her head. "Orders."

I considered that as I rinsed the last of the sandsoap from my hair and twisted it to get the water out. Orders from whom? Once again my mind filled with recent memories. More awake now, I knew that the rescue at Chovilun had been no dream. Was it possible that the Marquis had seen the justice of our cause and had switched sides? The escort, the humane treatment—surely that meant I was being sent home. Once again I felt relief and gratitude. As soon as I got to the castle I'd write a fine letter of thanks. No, I'd get Oria to write down my words, I decided, picturing the elegant Marquis. At least as embarrassing as had been the idea of waking up in his arms again was the idea of his trying to read my terrible handwriting and worse spelling.

"Don't stay in too long, my lady."

The voice recalled me to the present—and I realized my skin was getting chilled. Reluctantly I climbed out of the pool. At once my various aches and pains clamored for attention, and all I wanted to do was lie there in the sun and sleep forever.

But then delicious smells wafted from the other side of the rise, which woke up my appetite. Wringing out my hair, I hastily put on the clothes Yora Nessaren had laid out. They were hopelessly large on me—and when she saw it, she bit her lip, hard, in a praiseworthy attempt not to laugh. I looked down, saw the three stars that should have been in the middle of my chest resting over my stomach. I shook my head. "This is better than the dress?" I asked as she packed up the extra gear.

"Well, it's clean," she said, "and we'll belt it up. But when we ride, it's nine equerries for House Renselaeus that people will be seeing, my lady."

I was too tired to wonder what this meant—except I knew it was no immediate threat to me. So without asking any further questions, I followed her back over the rise to where a young man with two red braids tied back had laid out a little camp. In the distance I saw the horses being tended as they drank from the stream that fed my pool, but the others were nowhere in sight.

"Here, Lady Meliara." Yora Nessaren tossed me a carved shell comb.

As I attacked my hair she cut my old dress up and burned it bit by bit. I thought of Ara and was sorry to see it used thus.

The young man finished his preparations, then said, "All ready, Ness."

Just then the equerries who had been tending the horses came through the trees and sat down.

The riding captain looked at them, said, "We'll eat, then rotate positions so the others can have their meal. Then we're on the road."

Which is what happened. The red-haired young man, Amol, handed me a toasted length of bread that turned out to have meat, cheese, and greens stuffed into it. He also gave me a generous tin of tea, all without looking directly at me.

I sat on a rock with my hair hanging down to the grass all around me, drying in the warm breeze. The equerries ate quickly, with a minimum of conversation, and they studiously ignored me. When Nessaren and her group finished, they went by twos to replace the ones doing guard duty. Then everyone helped clean up. I was still working on my braid when they began to remount, and then I saw that there was a ninth horse. But Nessaren looked from me to it, frowning, then said, "We'll proceed as we started, I think, if you don't object, my lady." And bowed without a trace of ironic intent.

I knew I was too weak to ride on my own, and I realized I was not uncomfortable with the idea of riding with her on the same horse. So I just shrugged, finished my braid at last, wrapped it hastily around my head, and tucked the end under. One of them silently handed me a helm.

Nessaren was smiling faintly as she boosted me up onto her mount, but she said nothing beyond, "Ride out."

The others fell into formation, and away we went.

And that was the pattern for several days. The second day Nessaren offered me that last horse, which, of course, I accepted. We rode at a steady pace, occasionally cantering when the horses were fresh.

139

The first few times I rode alone I felt inordinately weary toward the end of each ride. But just when it seemed I was going to fall off, we'd make a stop for food and water, or to camp.

They had an extra bedroll for me, and we slept under the stars, or in a tent when it rained. We always stopped near a stream so that we could start our ride with a proper morning bath. We also stopped once at midday, when a hard rainstorm overtook us, and camped through the duration.

A time or two a pair of the riders would peel off and disappear, to reappear later with fresh supplies, or once with a sealed letter, which was given into Yora Nessaren's hands. She got that the day we stopped for the rainstorm, and since I had nothing else to do, I watched her read it.

As usual she said nothing, but she looked over at me with a faintly puzzled expression that I found disturbing because I couldn't interpret it.

Yora and the others were all scrupulously polite, and until that day, carefully distant. We had a big tent in which six or seven could sleep more or less comfortably. Four of them were in the tent with me, the rest busy with either the horses or guarding.

Nessaren sat cross-legged on her bedroll, tapping her letter against her knee. Finally she looked up. "Red, you and Snap go into Bularc. Falshalith is in charge of the garrison there—report in, say you've been on the search up in the hills and you want an update."

The red-haired fellow fingered the gold ring in his ear, then frowned. He glanced at me, then his gaze slid away. He said, "Think they'll talk?"

The woman they called Snap twiddled her fingers. "Why not? The more ignorant we are, the more Falshalith will condescend." Her brown eyes widened with false innocence. "After all, we're just servants, right?"

Snap and the redhead both looked at me; then she looked away and Amol said, "More tea, my lady?"

"No, thanks." I considered my next words.

For those first days it had taken all my energy just to keep up and not embarrass myself. But the regular food, and the rest, had restored a lot of my energy, and with it came curiosity.

I said tentatively, "You know, I have one or two questions..."

Amol's eyelids lifted like he was thinking, *Just one or two?* and Snap took her underlip firmly between her teeth. She seemed to have the quickest temper, but she was also the first to laugh. Both of them turned expectantly to their captain, who said calmly, "Please feel free to ask, Lady Meliara. I'll answer what I can."

"Well, first, there's that dungeon. Now, don't think I'm complaining, but the last thing I remember is Shevraeth's knife coming between me and a hot poker, you might say. I wake up with you, and we're on the road, going north. Remalna-city is south. I take it I'm not on my way back to being a guest of Greedy Galdran?"

Snap's head dropped quickly at the nickname for the King, as if to hide her laughter, but Amol snickered openly.

"No, my lady," Nessaren said.

"Well, then, it seems to me we're just about to the border. If we're going to Tlanth, we ought to be turning west."

"We are not going to Tlanth, my lady."

I said with a deep feeling of foreboding, "Can you tell me where we *are* going?"

"Yes, my lady. Home. To Renselaeus."

Not home to me, I thought, but because they had been so decent, I bit the comment back and just shook my head. "Why?"

"I do not know that. My orders were to bring you as quickly as was comfortable for you to travel."

"I'd like to go home," I said, polite as it was possible for me to be.

Nessaren's expression blanked, and I knew she was about to tell me I couldn't.

I said quickly, "It's not far. I just want to see my brother, and let him know what has happened to me. He must be worried—he might even think me dead."

At the words *my brother* her eyes flickered, but otherwise there was no change in her expression. When I was done speaking she said quietly, with a hint of regret, "I am sorry, my lady. I have my orders."

I tried once again. "A message to Branaric, then? Please. You can read it—you can *write* it—"

She shook her head once, her gaze not on me, but somewhere beyond the trees. We'd ceased to be companions, even in pretense—which left only enemies. "We're to have no communication with anyone outside of our own people," she said.

My first reaction was disbelief. Then I thought of that letter of thanks I'd planned on writing, and even though I had not told anyone, humiliation burned through me, followed by anger all the more bright for the sense of betrayal that underlay it all. Why betrayal? Shevraeth had never pretended to be on my side. Therefore he had saved my life purely for his own ends. Worse, my brother was somehow involved with his plans; I remembered Nessaren's subtle reaction to his mention, and I wondered if there had been some sort of reference to Bran in that letter Nessaren had just received. What else could this mean but that I was again to be used to force my brother to surrender?

Fury had withered all my good feelings, but I was determined not to show any of it, and I sat with my gaze on my hands, which were gripped in my lap, until I felt that I had my emotions under control again.

When I realized that the silence had grown protracted, I looked up and forced a polite smile. "I don't suppose you know where your Marquis is?" I asked, striving for a tone of nonchalance.

A quick exchange of looks, then Nessaren said, "I cannot tell you exactly, for I do not know, but he said that if you were to ask, I was to tender his compliments and regrets, but say events required him to move quickly."

And we're not? I thought about us waiting out the rain, and those nice picnics, and realized that Nessaren had been watching me pretty carefully. It was no accident that we'd stopped for rests, then;

Nessaren had very accurately gauged my strength. A fast run would have meant riding through rain and through nights, stopping only to change horses. We hadn't even had to do that.

Once again my emotions took a spin. I had had a taste of the way prisoners could be conveyed when the Baron had me thrown over a saddle for the trip to Chovilun. Nessaren and her riding had made certain that my journey so far was as pleasant as they could make it.

Is this, I wondered acidly, *possibly an attempt to win me to Shevraeth's side in whatever game he's playing with the King and the Baron?* Just the thought made me wild to face their Marquis once again and give him the benefit of my opinions.

But none of this could be shown now, I told myself. My quarrel was not with Nessaren and the equerries, who were just following orders. It was with their leader.

I glanced up, saw that they seemed to be waiting. For a reaction?

"Anyone know a good song?" I asked.

SIXTEEN

Turned out this was just the right question. Of the eight of them four played musical instruments, and Amol had a wonderful singing voice. They carried their instruments in their saddlebags, but in deference to me had not brought them out. After I made it clear I liked music, we had singing every night, and sometimes during long stretches of lonely country where no one else was about.

A lot of the songs were in Rensare, the very old dialect that apparently most of the people in the principality spoke. I knew little about Renselaeus, other than that it *was* a principality, a wealthy one, and for centuries had owed its allegiance directly to the Empire of Charas al Kherval, and only the most nominal allegiance to Remalna. Apparently one of our kings in the more recent past had won some kind of concessions from the Renselaeus ruler, and in turn the Renselaeans had been granted the county of Shevraeth, which lay on the coast in Remalna proper, hard against their southern border. This title went to the Renselaeus heir. The only things I knew about the Prince and Princess were that they were old, and that they had had a single heir late in life, the present Marquis.

My companions couldn't hide their surprise at my ignorance, but after I asked a few questions about the background of the songs, they started telling me about the homes, and life, and history there. And though they assiduously stayed away from the vexing topic of current events, I garnered a few interesting facts—not just about their loyalty to the Renselaeus family instead of to the Merindar crown, but the fact that the principality seemed to have its own army. A very well trained one, too.

This became really clear when Amol and Jamni returned from their mission. Both were excited, Amol laughing. "Report went to the King that the mysterious attack on Chovilun was by mountain raiders," he said.

"So my lord must have been right about those greens." Flerac pulled thoughtfully at his thin mustache. *Greens*, I'd gathered, was their nickname for Galdran's warriors.

"I'm just glad we didn't have to kill them," Snap put in, rolling her eyes. "Those two in the dungeon were sick as old oatmeal about being ordered to stand duty during torture. I can tell when someone's haystacking, and they weren't."

"What happened?" I asked, trying to hide my surprise. "I take it there was fighting when you people pulled me out of that Merindar fortress?"

They all turned to me, then to Nessaren, who said, "Some. We let some of them go, on oath they'd desert. There are plenty of greens who didn't want to join, or wish they hadn't."

"What about that lumping snarlface of a Baron?" I kept my voice as casual as possible, wondering what all this meant. Was Shevraeth, or was he not, Debegri's ally? "I hope he got trounced."

"He ran." Flerac's lip curled. "Came out, found his two bodyguards down, got out through some secret passage while we were trying to get in through another door. Don't think he saw any of us. Don't know, though."

Then they were no longer allies. What did *that* mean? Was Shevraeth trying to take Debegri's place in Galdran's favor?

"Report could be false," Amol said soberly.

Nessaren nodded once. "Let's pick up our feet, shall we?"
By which they meant it was time to ride faster.

As we made our way steadily northward, their spirits lifted at the prospect of home, and leave-time to enjoy it. From remarks they let fall it seemed that the Marquis had had them on duty day and night, with no breaks, during all the days of my run for freedom.

I really liked Nessaren and her riding. With good-natured generosity they treated me as a companion rather than as a prisoner. The last four mornings they even let me run through their morning sword drills with them. Some of it I knew from our own exercises with Khesot, but they had far better ones. I did my best to memorize the new material for taking back to our people in Tlanth.

The problem was, I realized as we raced across the northern hills, I was still furious with their leader.

My duty was clear: I had to escape.

Our last night before crossing the border we spent in a well-stocked cave, tucked up high on a rocky hill near a waterfall. The roar of the water was soothing, and the moist, cool air felt great after a long, hot ride. Until we were settled in I didn't notice that we were seven instead of nine, but as no one seemed concerned, I realized that two of them—tired as they must have been—had ridden on ahead.

As I rolled up in my sleeping bag, I felt an intense wave of homesickness. How many times had I camped out in just such places, high up in Tlanth? The sounds and smells of home permeated my dreams, making me wake up in a restless mood.

I was still restless when we rode over the bridge that spanned the river border. Restless and angry and apprehensive by turns. Not long after we crossed the border we stopped at an outpost, and there changed horses. Nessaren and the others all wanted to ride flat out for the capital. I wasn't asked my opinion.

Don't think I wasn't on the watch for a chance to peel off, but if anything their formation was now even tighter around me. I don't think it was even conscious—but there it was, I had about as much chance of getting away from them as a lone chicken had from a family of foxes.

Our road skirted a city built against a mountain. I caught glimpses of the terraced capital between cultivated hills. At the highest level was a castle, built on either side of a spectacular waterfall. A bridge lined with old trees crossed from one side to the other.

The castle slid out of sight as we rounded a hill and started up a road whose stones were worn smooth with age. Sentries in blue and black-and-white saluted us. I realized they thought I was one of them, and though no one even glanced twice at me, I felt more uncomfortable than ever.

After an uphill ride we emerged into a courtyard, horses' hooves clattering. The two members of the riding who'd left the night before came running out, along with several other people, all of them in the Renselaeus livery; some were in battle tunics, like Nessaren, and some in the shorter tunics and loose trousers of civilian wear.

Two of these latter came forward and for a moment they looked confused. With a smile—and accompanied by laughs from the others—Yora Nessaren indicated me. The two servants bowed. "Will you honor us by following this way, my lady?"

Behind me the others were chattering happily, exchanging news as they unloaded the horses. Soon they were out of earshot, and once again I walked with silent servants up a hallway. They were on either side of me, just out of reach, which diminished my chances of tripping them and scooting away. *All right, then*, I decided, *I will just have to make my break after whatever unpleasant interview is awaiting me.*

The hallway led to a circular stairway with two or three doors at each landing. Round four or five times upward, then we entered a very different type of hallway. Instead of the usual stone, or the tile of the wealthy, the floors were of exceptionally fine mosaic in a complicated pattern; but that only drew my eye briefly. Along one wall were high, arched windows whose diamond-shaped panes of clear glass looked out onto the terraced city below. It was an impressive sight.

At the end of the hall we trod up more stairs, wide, shallow, and tiled, passing beneath a domed glass ceiling. Around me small, carefully tended trees grew in pots.

Beyond those to another hall, with four doors—not woven doors, but real colorwood ones—redwood, bluewood, goldwood, greenwood—beautifully carved and obviously ancient.

The servants opened one and bowed me into a round-walled room that meant we were in a tower; windows on three sides looked out over the valley. The room was flooded with light, so much that I was dazzled for a moment and had to blink. Shading my eyes, I had a swift impression of a finely carved and gilded redwood table surrounded by blue satin cushions. Then I saw that the room was occupied.

Standing between two of the windows, almost hidden by slanting rays of sun, was a tall figure with pale blond hair.

The Marquis was looking down at the valley, hands clasped behind him. At the sound of the door closing behind me he looked up and came forward, and for a moment was a silhouette in the strong sunlight.

I stood with my back to the door. We were alone.

"Welcome to Renselaeus, Lady Meliara." And when I did not answer, he pointed to a side table. "Would you like anything to drink? To eat?"

"Why am I here?" I asked in a surly voice, suddenly and acutely aware of how ridiculous I must look dressed in his livery. "You may as well get the threats out at once. All this politeness seems about as false as..." *As a courtier's word*, I thought, but speech wouldn't come and I just shook my head.

He returned no immediate answer; instead seemed absorbed in

pouring wine from a fine silver decanter into two jewel-chased goblets. One he held out silently to me.

I wanted to refuse, but I needed somewhere to look and something to do with my hands, and I thought hazily that maybe the wine would clear my head. All of the emotions of the past days seemed to be fighting for prominence in me, making rational thought impossible.

He raised his cup in salute and took a drink. "Would you like to sit down?" He indicated the table. The light fell on the side of his face, and, like on that first morning after we came down from the mountain, I saw the marks of fatigue under his eyes.

"No," I said, and gulped some wine to fortify myself. "Why aren't you getting on with the sinister speeches?" I had started off with plenty of bravado, but then a terrible thought occurred, and I squawked, "Bran—"

"No harm has come to your brother," he said, looking up quickly. "I am endeavoring to find the best way to express—"

Having finished the wine, I slammed the goblet down onto a side table, and to hide my sudden fear—for I didn't believe him— I said as truculently as possible, "If you're capable of simple truth, just spit it out."

"Your brother has agreed to a truce," the Marquis started.

"Truce? What do you mean, a 'truce'?" I snarled. "He wouldn't surrender, he *wouldn't,* unless you forced him by threats to me—"

"I have issued no threats. It was only necessary to inform him that you were on your way here. He agreed to join us, for purposes of negotiation—"

A sun seemed to explode behind my eyes. "You've got Bran? *You used me to get my brother?*"

"He's here," the Marquis said, but he didn't get any further.

Giving a wail of sheer rage, I plucked a heavy silver candleholder and flung it straight at his head.

SEVENTEEN

HE CAUGHT IT ONE-HANDED, SET IT GENTLY BACK
in its place.

I clenched my teeth together to keep from screaming.

The Marquis stepped to the door, opened it. "Please bring
Lord Branaric here."

Then he sat down in one of the window seats and looked out
as though nothing had happened. I turned my back and glared out
the other window, and a long, terrible silence drained my wits entirely until the door was suddenly thrust open by an impatient hand;
and there was my brother, tall, thinner than I remembered, and
clean. "Mel!" he exclaimed.

"Bran," I squawked, and hurled myself into his arms.

After a moment of incoherent questions on my part, he patted
my back then held me out at arm's length. "Here, Mel, what's this?
You look like death's cousin! Where'd you get that black eye? And
your hands—" He turned over my wrists, squinting down at the
healing rope burns. "Curse it, what's toward?"

"Debegri," I managed, laughing and crying at once. "Oh, Bran,
that's not the worst of it. Look at this!" I stuck out my bare foot
to show the purple scars. "That horrid trap—"

"We pulled 'em all out," he said, and grimaced. "It was the

Hill Folk sent someone to tell us about you—that's a first, and did it scare me!—but by the time we got down the mountain, you were gone. I'm sorry, Mel. You were right."

"I was s-s-s-*stupid*. I got caught, and now we're both in trouble," I wailed into his shoulder.

The carved door snicked shut, and I realized we were alone. I gave a great sob that seemed to come up from my dusty bare toes, and all those pent-up emotions stormed out. Bran sighed and just held me for a long time, until at last I got control again and pulled away, hiccoughing. "T-Tell me how everyone is, and what happened?"

"Khesot, Julen, both are fine. Hrani cut up bad, but coming through. We lost young Omic and two of those Faluir villagers. That was when we tried a couple of runs on the greenie camp. Afterward, though, we got up Debegri's nose but good," he said with a grin. "Ho! I don't like to remember those early days. Our people were absolutely wild, mostly mad at me about those accursed traps. After our second run, Shevraeth sent a warning under truce. Said you were on your way to Remalna-city, and we should hole up against further communication. Then we found out that the King had gone off on one of his tantrums—apparently wasn't best pleased to find that this fop of a marquis had done better in two weeks than his cousin had in two months, and gave the command back to Debegri. We enjoyed that." He grinned again, then winced. "Until Azmus appeared. Nearly killed himself getting to our camp. Told us about the King's threat, and your escape, and that you'd disappeared and he couldn't find you. Debegri left, with half his army, and we knew it was to search for you. We waited for word. Bad time, there."

"*You* think it was bad . . . " I started.

"Mmm." He hugged me again. "Tell me."

Vivid images chased through my mind: Shevraeth over the campfire; Galdran's throne room and that horrible laughter; the escape; what Ara's mother said; that fortress. I didn't know how to begin, so I shook my head and said, "Never mind it now. Tell me more."

He shrugged, rubbing his jaw. "Shevraeth sent us a message about six days ago, white flag, said he had you and wanted to discuss the situation with me—on our ground. He knew where we were! And next morning, there *they* were. We met at the Whitestream bridge. His people on one side, ours on the other. I was itchy as two cats with fleas, afraid one or the other side would let loose on either me *or* him and either way there'd be blood for certain. He strolled out like it was a ballroom floor, cool as you please, said you were safe in his care—what's that?"

"I said, 'Hah!' "

He grinned. "Well, anyhow, he told me that Debegri was promised not just our lands but a dukedom if he could flush us out once and for all. Baron plans to fire us out, soon's the rains end. Shevraeth promised safe passage to and from Renselaeus—on his word—if I came along with him for a talk. He told me you were on your way, and said if I came, whatever we decided, you could return to Tlanth with me. Didn't see any way around it, so—" He lifted his hands. "Here I am. Rode all day two days, and all night last night, got here this morning. Must say, he's been decent enough—"

"I *hate* him and those Court smirkers!" I cried. "Hate, hate, hate—"

The door opened behind us, and we both whirled around rather guiltily.

A servant appeared, bowed, said, "My lord, my lady, His Highness Prince Alaerec requests the honor of your company at dinner. Should you wish to prepare, we are instructed to provide everything necessary."

Bran chuckled. "Wait until you see the bath they have here! One of these ice-faced Renselaeus toffs has to have been thick as thieves with a first-rate mage. No lowly bathhouses for this gang."

My face felt like a flame by then, but Bran didn't notice. "I'll

152

have a little of that wine while you go on," he added, rubbing his hands.

This left me with nothing to do but follow the servant back down the hall and down one level of stairs to another hall. He opened a door, bowed, waited until I passed him, then closed the door again.

This left me in a room I had never seen anything even remotely like.

It reminded me of a stream in a forest. Trees grew alongside a wide running bath, all tiled and blue and clean. High windows let in clear light. *Magic, indeed,* I thought as I moved to the edge of the eddying water, I dipped a hand in, found that it was warm. *Lots of magic.*

A quiet rustle brought my head around; three maidservants gowned in blue and white came forward, bowed; and one said, "My lady, His Highness sends his compliments and begs you to make use of Her Highness's wardrobe."

I thought of that imperious voice at the palace and tried not to laugh. The change from oversized livery to an elderly lady's court frills and furbelows would probably manage to make me look more ridiculous than ever. But what alternative was there? My own clothes—such as they were—had been burned by Ara's mother a long time ago.

As soon as I was in that bath, though, these thoughts, and most of my other worries, were soothed away from my mind as the various aches were soothed from my body. It felt as if I were sitting in a rushing stream; only, the water was warm, and soft as finespun silk, and the soaps were subtly scented and made my skin glow. Everything was laid out for me, from comb to teeth cleaner.

There was even a salve to work through one's hair, one of the maids pointed out. She did it for me (which almost put me right to sleep, tired as I was) and afterward, the comb seemed to slide right through my hair.

Then, wrapped in a cape-sized towel that had been kept warm

on heatstones, I followed the maids into an adjacent room as large as the bath. There were trunks and trunks of fabrics of every type and hue.

Feeling like a trespasser, I fingered through the nearest, stopping when I saw a gown of green velvet. Tiny golden birds had been embroidered at the neck and down either side of the bodice laces. The sleeves, unlike the present fashions, were narrow, and embroidered at the cuffs. Tiny slits had been made at shoulders and elbows to pull through tufts of the silken underdress of pale gold. The fabrics whispered richly as the maids helped me to pull them on without tangling my hair, which hung, wet and free, to my knees. When the overdress settled around me, I discovered that the Princess was not much larger than I, which made me want to laugh.

Someone brought slippers, and I thought of Julen as I put them on and laced them. They were tight—the Princess obviously had tiny feet—but they were so soft it didn't much matter. Certainly they fit better than the outgrown mocs I'd gotten from the blacksmith's son.

When the gown was laced and the sleeves adjusted, one of the maids brought out a mirror. I looked in surprise at myself; the gown made me look taller, but nothing could make me seem larger. My face looked *old* to my eyes, and kind of grim, the black eye ridiculous.

I turned away quickly. "I'm ready. Where is my brother?"

In answer one of the maids bowed and scurried out the door, her steps soundless on the tiles. One of the others bore away Nessaren's clothes, and the third opened a door for me and bowed; and I walked through, feeling like a real fool. I was afraid I'd forget about the train dragging behind me, trip, and go rolling down the stairs, so I grabbed fistfuls of skirt at either side and walked carefully after her.

"Ho, Mel! You look like you're treading on knives." Branaric's voice came from behind me.

"Well, I don't want to ruin this gown. Isn't mine," I said.

He just grinned, and we were led down another level to an elegant room with a fire at one end and windows looking out over the valley. The sun was setting, and the scene below was bathed in the rosy-golden light.

We went forward. There were cushioned benches on either side of the fire, and directly before it a great carved chair. Shevraeth rose from one of the benches, making a gesture of welcome. Indicating the chair, in which sat a straight-backed old man dressed in black velvet, he said, "Father, I have the honor of introducing Lady Meliara Astiar." And to me, in the suavest voice, as if I hadn't flung a candleholder at his head just a little while before, "Lady Meliara, my father, Prince Alaerec."

The old man nodded slowly and with great dignity. He had keen dark eyes, and white hair which he wore loose on his shoulders in the old-fashioned way. "My dear, please forgive me if I do not rise. I am afraid I do not get about with ease or grace anymore."

I felt an impulse to bow, and squashed it. I remembered that Court women sweep curtsys—something my mother had tried once to teach me, when I was six. I also remembered that I was there against my will—a prisoner, despite all the fine surroundings and polite talk—so I just crossed my arms and said, "Don't think you have to walk about on my behalf."

Bran gave me a slightly bemused look and bobbed an awkward bow to the old man.

A servant came forward, silent and skillful, and passed out goblets of wine. The Prince saluted me in silence, followed by Bran and Shevraeth. I looked down at my goblet, then took a big gulp that made my nose sting.

In a slow, pleasant voice, Prince Alaerec asked mild questions —weather, travel, Bran's day and how he'd filled it. I stayed silent as the three of them worked away at this limping conversation. The Renselaeus father and son were skilled enough at nothing-talk, but poor Bran stumbled over half his words, sending frequent glances at me. In the past I'd often spoken for both of us, for truth was he

155

felt awkward with his tongue and was somewhat shy with new people, but I did not feel like speaking until I'd sorted my emotions out—and there was no time for that.

To bridge his own feelings, my brother gulped at the very fine wine they offered. Soon a servant came in and announced that dinner was ready, and the old Prince rose slowly, leaning heavily on a cane. His back was straight, though, as he led the way to a dining room. Bran and I fell in behind, I treading cautiously, with my skirts bunched in either hand.

Bran snickered. I looked up, saw him watching me, his face flushed. "Life, Mel, are you supposed to walk like that?" He snickered again, swallowed the rest of his third glass of wine, then added, "Looks like you got eggs in those shoes."

"I don't *know* how I'm supposed to walk," I mumbled, acutely aware of that bland-faced, elegantly dressed Marquis right behind us, and elbowed Bran in the side. "Stop laughing! If I drop these skirts, I'll trip over them."

"Why didn't you just ask for riding gear?"

"And a coach-and-six while I was at it? This is what they *gave* me."

"Well, it looks right enough," he admitted, squinting down at me. "It's just—seeing you in one of those fancy gowns reminds me of—"

I didn't want to hear what it reminded him of. "You're drunk as four skunks, you idiot," I muttered, and not especially softly, either. "You'd best lay it aside until you get some food into you."

He sighed. "Right enough. I confess, I didn't think you'd really get here—thought that there'd be another bad hit."

"Well, I don't see we're all that safe yet," I said under my breath.

The dining room was formidably elegant—I couldn't take it in all at once. A swift glance gave the impression of the family colors, augmented by gold, blended with artistry and grace. The table was high, probably to accommodate the elderly Prince. The chairs, one for each diner, were especially fine—no angles, everything curves and ovals and pleasing lines.

The meal, of course, was just as good. Again I left the others to work at a polite conversation. I bent my attention solely to my food, eating a portion of every single thing offered, until at last—and I never thought it would happen again, so long it had been—I was truly stuffed.

This restored to me a vestige of my customary good spirits, enough so that when the Prince asked me politely if the dinner had been sufficient, and if he could have anything else brought out, I smiled and said, "It was splendid. Something to remember all my life. But—" I realized I was babbling, and shut up.

The Prince's dark eyes narrowed with amusement, though his mouth stayed solemn—I knew I'd seen that expression before. "Please. You have only to ask."

"I don't want a thing. It was more a question, and that is: If you can eat like this every day, why aren't you fatter than five oxen?"

Bran set his goblet down, his eyes wide. "Burn it, Mel, I was just thinking the very same!"

That was the moment I realized that, though our rank was as high as theirs, or nearly, and our name as old, Branaric and I must have sounded as rustic and ignorant as a pair of backwoods twig gatherers. It ruined my mood. I put my fork down and scrutinized the Prince for signs of the sort of condescending laughter that would—no doubt—make this a rich story to pass around Court as soon as we were gone.

Prince Alaerec said, "During my peregrinations about the world, I discovered some surprising contradictions in human nature. One of them is that, frequently anyway, the more one has, the less one desires."

His voice was mild and pleasant, and impossible to divine any direct meaning from. I turned for the first time to his son, to meet that same assessing gaze I remembered from our first encounter. How long had *that* been trained on me?

Now thoroughly annoyed, I said, "Well, if you're done listening to us sit here and make fools of ourselves, why don't we get on to whatever it is you're going to hold over our heads next?"

Neither Renselaeus reacted. It was Bran who blinked at me in surprise and said, "Curse it, Mel, where are your wits at? Didn't Shevraeth tell you? We're part of their plan to kick Galdran off his throne!"

EIGHTEEN

"WHAT?" I YELLED. AND I OPENED MY MOUTH TO
complain *Nobody told me anything*, but I recalled a certain interview,
not long ago, that had ended rather abruptly when a candleholder
had—ah—changed hands. Grimacing, I said in a more normal
voice, "When did this happen?"

"That's the joke on us." Bran laughed. "They've been at it as
long as we have. Longer, even."

I looked from father to son and read nothing in those bland,
polite faces. "Then . . . why . . . didn't you respond to our letter?"

As I spoke the words, a lot of things started making sense.

I thought back to what Ara's father had said, and then I remembered Shevraeth's words about the purpose of a court. When
I glanced at Prince Alaerec, he saluted me with his wineglass; just
a little gesture, but I read in it that he had comprehended a good
deal of my thoughts.

Which meant that *my* face, as usual, gave me away—and of
course this thought made my cheeks burn.

He said, "We admire—tremendously—your courageous efforts
to right the egregious wrongs obtaining in Remalna."

Thinking again of Ara's father and Master Kepruid the innkeeper, I said, "But the people don't welcome armies trampling

through their houses and land, even armies on their side. I take it you've figured out some miraculous way around this?"

Bran slapped his palm down on the table. "That's it, Mel—where we've been blind. We were trying to push our way in from without, but Shevraeth, here, has been working from within." He nodded in the Prince's direction. "Both—all three of 'em, in fact."

I blinked, trying to equate with a deadly plot an old, imperious voice whose single purpose seemed to be the safety of her clothing. "The Princess is part of this, too?"

"She is the one who arranged your escape from Athanarel," Shevraeth said to me. "The hardest part was finding your spy."

"You knew about Azmus?"

"I knew you had to have had some kind of contact in Remalna-city, from some of the things you said during our earlier journey. We had no idea who, or what, but we assumed that this person would display the same level of loyalty your compatriots had when you first fell into our hands, and I had people wait to see who might be lurking around the palace, watching."

Questions crowded my thoughts. But I pushed them all aside, focusing on the main one. "If you're rebelling, then you must have someone in mind for the throne. Who?"

Bran pointed across the table at Shevraeth. "He seems to want to do it, and I have to say, he'd be better at it than I."

"No, he wouldn't," I said without thinking.

Bran winced and rubbed his chin. "Mel..."

"Please, my dear Lord Branaric," the Prince murmured. "Permit the lady to speak. I am interested to hear her thoughts on the matter."

Rude as I'd been before, my response had shocked even me, and I hadn't intended to say anything more. Now I sneaked a peek at the Marquis, who just sat with his goblet in his fingers, his expression one of mild questioning.

I sighed, short and sharp. "You'd be the best because you *aren't* Court trained," I said to Bran. It was easier than facing those other

160

two. "Court ruined, I'd say. You don't lie—you don't even know how to lie in social situations like this. I think it's time the kingdom's leader is known for honesty and integrity, not for how well he gambles or how many new fashions he's started. Otherwise we'll just be swapping one type of bad king for another."

Bran drummed his fingers on the table, frowning. "But I don't want to do it. Not alone, anyway. If you are with me—"

"I'm not going to Remalna-city," I said quickly.

All three of them looked at me—I could feel it, though I kept my own gaze on my brother's face. His eyes widened. I said, "You're the one who always wanted to go there. I've been. Once. It's not an experience I'd care to repeat. You'd be fine on your own," I finished weakly, knowing that he wouldn't—that I'd just managed, through my own anger, to ruin his chances.

"Mel, I don't know what to say. Where t'start, burn it!" Bran ran his fingers through his hair, snarling it up—a sure sign he was upset. "Usually it's you with the quick mind, but this time I think you're dead wrong."

"On the contrary," the Prince said, with a glance at his son. "She makes cogent points. And there will be others aside from the loyalists in Tlanth who will, no doubt, share a similar lack of partisanship."

"Your point is taken, Father," Shevraeth said. "It is an issue that I will have to address."

Sensing that there was more meaning to their words than was immediately obvious, I looked from one to the other for clues, but of course there were none that I could descry.

Branaric filled his glass again. "So, what exactly is it you want from us?"

"Alliance," Shevraeth said. "How that will translate into practical terms is this: You withdraw to your home, to all appearances willing to negotiate a truce. I shall do my best to prevail upon Galdran to accept this truce, and we can protract it on technicalities for as long as may be, which serves a double purpose—"

161

"End the fighting, but honorably," Bran said, nodding. "I understand you so far. What if Debegri comes after us anyway?"

"In apprehension of that, my people are taking and holding the Vesingrui fortress on your border. For now they are wearing the green uniform, as servants of the Crown. If Debegri goes on the attack, I will send this force against him. If not—"

"They'll leave us be?"

"Yes."

"And if Debegri doesn't come?"

"You wait. I hope to achieve the objective peacefully, or with as little unpleasantness as possible. If it transpires that I do require aid in the northwest, I would like to be able to rely on you and your people as a resource."

"And after?"

"As we discussed. Honor the Covenant. No more forced levies; tax reform; trade reestablished with the outside, minus the tariffs that went into the Merindar personal fortune. That's to start."

Bran shrugged, rubbed his hands from his jaw to through his hair, then he turned to me. "Mel?"

"I would prefer to discuss it later," I said.

"What's to discuss?" Bran said, spreading his hands.

"The little matter of the crown," Shevraeth said dryly. "If we are finished, I propose we withdraw for the evening. We are all tired and would do the better for a night's sleep."

I turned to him. "You said to Bran we can leave, whatever we decide."

He bowed.

"Good. We'll leave in the morning. First light."

Bran's jaw dropped.

"I want to go home," I said fiercely.

The Prince must have given some signal undiscernible to me, for suddenly a servant stood behind my chair, to whom Prince Alaerec said, "Please conduct the Countess to the chamber prepared for her."

I got up, said to Bran, "I'll need something to wear on the ride home."

He slewed around in his chair. "But—"

I said even more fiercely than before, "Do you really think I ought to wear *this* home—even if it were mine, which it isn't?"

"All right." Branaric rubbed his eyes. "Curse it, I can't think for this headache on me. Maybe I'd better turn in myself."

He fell in step beside me and we were led out. I walked with as much dignity as I could muster, holding that dratted skirt out away from my feet. My shoulder blades itched; I imagined the two Renselaeuses staring, and I listened for the sound of their laughter long after we'd traversed the hall and gone up a flight of stairs.

I slept badly.

It wasn't the fault of the room, which was charmingly furnished, or the bed, which was softer than anything I'd ever slept on. And it wasn't as if I weren't tired, for I was. After restless tossing half the night, I decided I just needed—desperately—to be home, and I rose and sat in the window seat to look up at the stars.

I fell asleep there at last, and didn't waken until a maid came in. She looked slightly surprised at seeing me sitting in the window in my borrowed nightgown, my head on my knees, but said nothing beyond, "Good morning, my lady." Then she bowed and laid a bundle on the bed. "His Highness requests the honor of your company at breakfast, whenever you are ready. Do you need anything?"

"No. Thanks."

She bowed again and withdrew.

After another bath in that wondrous room I put on the clothes the maid had brought, which turned out to be an old shirt, that green tunic Hrani had remade for Branaric, now considerably the worse for a winter's wear, and some trousers. I had to use the laces from the shirt to belt up the trousers, and the sleeves were much

163

too long, making awkward rolls at my wrists, but the outsized tunic covered it all.

I was just brushing my hair out when there was a quick knock at the door. Branaric came in. "Ready?"

"Nearly," I said, my fingers quickly starting the braid. "I suppose you don't have extra gloves, or another hat?" I eyed the battered object he held in his hand. "No, obviously not. Well, I can ride bareheaded. Who's to see me that I care about?"

He smiled briefly, then gave me a serious look. "Are you certain you don't want to join the alliance?"

"Yes."

He sank down heavily onto the bed and pulled from his tunic a flat-woven wallet. "I don't know, Mel. What's toward? You wouldn't even listen yesterday, or hardly. Isn't like you, burn it!"

"I don't trust these cream-voiced courtiers as far as I can spit into a wind," I said as I watched him pull from the wallet a folded paper. "And I don't see why we should risk any of our people, or our scarce supplies, to put one of them on the throne. If he wants to be king, let him get it on his own."

Bran sighed, his fingers working at the shapeless brim of his hat. "I think you're wrong."

"You're the one who was willed the title," I reminded him. "I'm not legally a countess—I haven't sworn anything at Court. Which means it's just a courtesy title until *you* marry. You can do whatever you want, and you have a legal right to it."

"I know all that. Why are you telling me again? I remember we both promised when Papa died that we'd be equals in war and in peace. You think I'll renege, just because we disagree for the first time? If so, you must think me as dishonest as you paint them." He jerked his thumb back at the rest of the Renselaeus palace. I could see that he was upset.

"I don't question you, Bran. Not at all. What's that paper?"

Instead of answering, he tossed it to me. I unfolded it carefully, for it was so creased and battered it was obvious it had seen a great deal of travel. Slowly and painstakingly I puzzled out the words—then looked up in surprise. "This is Debegri's letter about the colorwoods!"

"Shevraeth asked about proof that the Merindars were going to break the Covenant. I brought this along, thinking that—if we were to join them—they could use it to convince the rest of Court of Galdran's treachery."

"You'd *give* it to them?" I demanded.

Bran sighed. "I thought it a good notion, but obviously you don't. Here. You do whatever you think best. I'll bide by it." He dropped the wallet onto my lap. "But I wish you'd give them a fair listen."

I folded the letter up, slid it inside the waterproof wallet, and then put it inside my tunic. "I guess I'll have to listen to the father, at any rate, over breakfast." As I wrapped my braid around my head and tucked the end under, I added, "Which we'd better get to as soon as possible, so we have a full day of light on the road."

"You go ahead—it was you the Prince invited. I'll chow with Shevraeth. And be ready whenever you are."

It was with a great sense of relief that I went to the meal, knowing that I'd only have to face one of them. *And for the last time ever*, I vowed as the ubiquitous servants bowed me into a small dining room.

The Prince was already seated in a great chair. With a graceful gesture he indicated the place opposite him, and when I was seated, he said, "My wife will regret not having had a chance to meet you, Lady Meliara."

Wondering what this was supposed to mean, I opened my hands. I hoped it looked polite—I was not going to lie and say I wished I might have met her, for I didn't, even if it was true that she had aided my palace escape.

The door opened, and food was brought in and set before us. The last thing the server did was to pour a light brown liquid into

165

a porcelain cup. The smell was interesting, though I didn't recognize it.

"What is this?" I asked.

The servant had withdrawn. "Chocolate," said Prince Alaerec. "From the Summer Islands. I thought you might enjoy it."

I took a cautious taste, then a more enthusiastic one. "It's good!"

He smiled and indicated I was to help myself from the various chafing dishes set before us. Which I did, with a very liberal hand, for I didn't know when or where Bran and I would eat next.

When we were finished, the Prince said, "Have you any further questions concerning the matter we discussed last night?"

"One." While I felt no qualms about being rude to his son, I was reluctant to treat the elderly man the same. "You really have been planning this for a long time?"

"For most of my life."

"Then why didn't you respond? Offer to help us—at least offer a place in your alliance—when Bran and I sent our letter to the King at the start of winter?"

The Prince paused to take a sip of his coffee. I noted idly that he had long, slim hands like his son's. Had the Prince ever wielded a sword? *Oh yes—wasn't he wounded in the Pirate Wars?*

"There was much to admire in your letter," he said with a faint smile. "Your forthright attitude, the scrupulous care with which you documented each grievance, all bespoke an earnestness, shall we say, of intent. What your letter lacked, however, was an equally lucid plan for what to do after Galdran's government was torn down."

"But we did include one," I protested.

He inclined his head. "In a sense. Your description of what the government ought to be was truly enlightened. Yet... as the military would say, you set out a fine strategy, but failed to supplement it with any kind of tactical carry-through." His eyes narrowed slightly, and he added, "It is always easiest to judge where one is ignorant—a mistake we made about you, and that we have striven to correct—but it seemed that you and your adherents were idealistic and courageous, yet essentially foolhardy, folk. We were very much afraid you would not last long against the sheer weight of Galdran's army, its poor leadership notwithstanding."

I thought this over, looking for hidden barbs—and for hidden meanings.

He said, "If you should change your mind, or if you simply need to communicate with us, please be assured you shall be welcome."

It seemed that, after all, I was about to go free. "I confess I'll feel a lot more grateful for your kindness after I get home."

He set his cup down and steepled his fingers. "I understand," he murmured. "Had I lived through your recent experiences, I expect I might have a similar reaction. Suffice it to say that we wish you well, my child, whatever transpires."

"Thank you for that," I said awkwardly, getting to my feet.

He also rose. "I wish you a safe, swift journey." He bowed over my hand with graceful deliberation.

I left then, but for the first time in days I didn't feel quite so bad about recent events.

I found Bran in the courtyard below. Two fresh, mettlesome horses awaited us, and Bran had a bag at his belt. Shevraeth himself was there to bid us farewell—a courtesy I could have done without. Impatient to be gone, I stayed silent as he and my brother exchanged some last words.

Then, at last, Shevraeth stepped back. "Do you remember the route?"

Bran nodded. "Well enough. My thanks again—" He looked over at me, then sighed. "Another time, I trust." I realized then that he actually *liked* the Marquis—that in some wise (as much as a Court decoration and an honest man ill trained in the niceties of high society could) they had become friends.

Shevraeth turned to me, bowed. There was no irony visible in face or manner as he wished me a safe journey. I felt my face go hot as I gritted out a stilted "Thank you." Then I turned in my saddle and my horse spun about. Branaric was with me in a moment, and side-by-side we rode out.

And in silence we began our journey. The horses seemed to want speed, which gladdened my heart. I turned my back on the terraced city with its thundering fall; faced west and home.

We stopped at noon to rest the horses, and to eat the packet of food someone had given Bran while I was at breakfast. Sitting under a tree, dabbling my feet in a stream, I felt my restlessness wash away and my spirits soar. Branaric seemed unusually quiet. His face, customarily so good-humored, was somber.

"Cheer up," I said. "We'll soon be home."

He looked up, his bread half forgotten in his hand. "And forsworn."

A cold feeling went through me. "No." I shook my head. "Galdran will fall—*if* they're telling the truth—which is what Papa wanted."

"He wanted us to help, and to lend our strength to rebuilding afterward. Now we're to sit and watch it all from a distance." He looked down at his bread and pitched it across the stream, where a flock of noisy blue-plumaged tzillis squabbled over it. "Why do you persist in thinking they are liars? They haven't lied to me. What lies did they tell you?"

"Half-truths," I muttered. "Court-bred..."

"You keep plinking out that same tune, Mel, but the truth is—" He stopped, shook his head.

"Go ahead." The coldness in my middle turned to a sick feeling. "Get it out."

"No use." He shrugged. "If I were going to pitch into you, I ought to have done it last night, but it didn't seem fair to do it on their turf. Come on, let's go home." He climbed back onto his horse. I followed, and in silence once more we took to the road.

That night we stayed at an inn. We had good rooms, and an excellent meal, all paid for by Renselaeus beneficence. Bran's mood stayed somber even through the fine music of some wandering minstrels who played for the common room, and he went early to bed.

Enough of his mood lingered that, for the first time, I did not slip into the magical spell of music but listened with only part of my mind. The other part kept reviewing memories I would rather forget, and portions of conversations, until at last I gave up and went to my room. There I took out and puzzled my way through Debegri's entire letter, which made me angry all over again. I spent a very restless night.

Branaric woke me the next morning with an impatient knock. As soon as we'd bathed, dressed, and breakfasted, we were on the road, with new horses. Bad weather followed us; the wind chased coldly through the trees, and the air was heavy with the smell of impending rain. The edge of a storm caught us in the last afternoon, but we kept riding until sundown. It became apparent that Bran was looking for somewhere specific. We finally reached a small town and slowed until we rode into the courtyard of an inn on its market square.

This was just as the rain hit in earnest.

That night I lay in another clean bed, listening to the wind howl and a tree scratch at the window with twiggy fingers. It was a mournful, uncanny sound that disturbed my dreams.

The storm passed west and south just before dawn, leaving a cold, dripping world. Now we had reached the heavy forestland at the base of the mountains; by midday we would reach the lowest border of Tlanth.

Even Bran seemed slightly more cheery at the prospect of

getting home, and we both rose early and ate quickly, eager to get going.

Until that morning most of the journey had been made in silence, our stops to eat and change horses—again, Renselaeus beneficence: all we had to do was mention their name, and the horses were instantly available—too brief for much converse. When we did stop, we were both too tired to talk. But that day the roads were too muddy for fast travel, and Branaric suddenly turned to me and asked for my story, so I gave him a detailed description of my adventures.

I had just reached the episode at the fountain with Debegri, and was grinning at the fluency and point of Bran's curses, when we became aware of horses behind us.

Traffic had been nonexistent all day, which we had expected. No traders had been permitted to go up into Tlanth for months. We were on the southernmost road into Tlanth, well away from Vesingrui, the fortress that the Renselaeus forces supposedly held, so we didn't expect any military traffic, either.

"Sounds like at least one riding," I said, remembering that pattern well. Danger prickled along my nerves, and I wished I had a weapon.

"Something must have happened." Bran sounded unconcerned. "They must need to tell us—"

"Who? What?"

Bran shrugged. "Escort. Shevraeth sent it along to keep us safe. Knew you would refuse, so they've been behind us the whole way."

I was peering through the trees, anger and apprehension warring inside me. Annoyed as I was to be thus circumvented—and to have my reactions so accurately predicted—I realized I'd be well satisfied to find out that the approaching riders were indeed Renselaeus equerries.

The Renselaeus colors would have stood out, but the green-and-brown of Galdran's people blended into the forest; they were almost on us before we saw them, and Bran yelled, "It's a trap!"

"Halt!" The shout rang through the trees.

Of course we bolted.

"Halt, or we shoot," came a second yell.

"Bend down, bend—ah!"

Bran's body jerked, then he fell forward, an arrow in his back.

NINETEEN

OUR HORSES PLUNGED UP THE TRAIL.

"Go on...Go!" Bran jerked one hand toward the mountains, then swayed in his saddle.

Another arrow sang overhead.

"I won't leave you," I snapped.

"Go. Our people...Carry on the fight."

"Bran—"

In answer he yanked the reins on his terrified horse, which lunged toward mine. Gritting his teeth, he leaned out and whipped the ends of his reins across the mare's shoulder. "*Go!*"

My mount panicked, leaped forward. My neck snapped back. I clutched to the horse's mane with all my strength. The last glimpse I had of Bran was of his white face and his anxious eyes watching me as he and his mount fell back.

And then I was on my own.

For a time the mare raced straight up the trail while the only thought I could hold in my mind was, *A trap? A trap?* And then the image, seen endlessly, of Bran being shot.

Then a scrap of memory floated up before my inner eye. Again I saw the elegant Renselaeus dining room, heard the Marquis's refined drawling voice: *My people are taking and holding the Vesingrui fortress on your border. For now they are wearing the green uniform* . . .

A trap. Cold fury washed through me. *They have betrayed us.*

It was then that I recovered enough presence of mind to realize that I was in my home territory at last, and I could leave the trail anytime. The horse had recovered from the panic and was trotting. So I recaptured the reins, leading the horse across the side of the mountain toward the thickest, oldest part of the local forest. It didn't take me long to lose the pursuit, and then I turned my tired mare north, permitting her to slow as I thought everything through.

It made perfect sense, after all. Bran and I were certainly an inconvenience, especially since we'd refused to ally. For a moment guilt tweaked at my thoughts—if it hadn't been for me, we'd both be alive and well in their capital. And in their hands, I told myself. If they could cold-bloodedly plan this kind of treachery, wasn't this sort of end waiting for us anyway?

And now Bran is dead. Branaric, my fun-loving, trusting brother, the one who pleaded with me to give them a fair chance. Who wanted to be their friend.

All my emotions narrowed to one arrow of intent: revenge.

It was nightfall, under a heavy storm, when I reached Erkan-Astiar, home to my family for over five hundred years. I didn't even go to the castle, which looked dark and cold. I went straight to the smithy, and there found Julen and Calaub sitting down to tea and porridge.

Within a short time all our leaders were crowded together in their tiny kitchen. Celebration at my appearance was short-lived, for as soon as I had them together I told them what had happened, withholding no detail.

Anger—grief—fear—questions—disbelief: These were the reactions from our people. Some expressed a variety of these reactions, as questions and amplifications went back and forth.

Finally, there in the old smithy under a howling wind, I

formally set everyone free of the oath they'd sworn to Bran and me. "We can't win, not now," I said, with tears burning my eyes. "But those who want to take a few of them with us when we go down, come with me."

Devan gripped his club, glowering up at the ceiling. "We goin' against Vesingrui?"

I nodded, wiping my eyes on the sleeve of my tunic, wet as it was. "Supposedly they took it to watch for Debegri's soldiers, but I expect they're there to keep us divided from the rest of the kingdom. An all-out attack on that fortress will achieve something."

It was mostly the young—all Branaric's particular friends, and mine—who stepped forward. I said to them, "We'll leave as soon as you can get every weapon you can lay hold of. Choose only the experienced, surefooted mounts, for we'll travel all night and attack at dawn."

Khesot sat across from me at the table, silent, smoking his pipe. When everyone had left, some to get their weapons and others to go home, he squinted at me over the drifting silver smoke and said, "You ought to be certain you are right."

"I am."

He shook his head slowly.

"You don't believe me?" I demanded.

"I believe every word you have said, my lady," he murmured, his quiet tone a gentle reproof. "But there remain enough questions to make me feel that there might yet be another explanation."

"What else could there be? They were the only ones who knew where we were—and who."

He pursed his lips. "I swore I would stay with you until the end, whether victory or defeat, and so I will. But this seems a foolhardy death you lead our folk to. Let me propose this. I will come with you—and I expect others will follow, if I go—if you grant me one thing, an initial scouting party."

Instinct fought against common sense. My wish was to ride with steel in either hand to death and destruction, as quickly as possible.

Nothing, ever, could extinguish the terrible pain in my heart, except annihilation. But I had been raised to think of others, and so I forced myself to agree, though with no real grace.

He rose, bowed, and went out. I knelt there on Julen's soggy cushion, staring at my own hands wrapped around the squat mug I'd known since I was small. My hands looked like a stranger's, taut and white knuckled.

There was a quiet step, and I looked up.

"I saved this for you," said Oria, her pretty face unwontedly somber as she held out my short sword.

I took it, turned it over in my hands. "Are you coming with me?"

She looked over her shoulder. "Mama said I can do what I want. There are a lot of us whose families are arguing it out right now."

"I'm sorry," I said tightly, though I wasn't. *Go . . . our people . . . carry on the fight . . .* When I closed my eyes, I saw Bran's white, pain-grim face. I shook my head, resolving not to close my eyes again.

Oria dropped down on the cushion beside me. "I'd rather die tonight than live with—your brother gone, and us under Debegri's rule." She smiled sadly, her brown eyes shiny with unshed tears. "Why is it the songs all end with the good people winning, but in life they don't?"

"They don't make songs when the good lose," I muttered. "They make more war chants against the bad. So there won't be any songs for us." *Just laughter—*

Your brother has agreed to a truce. Shevraeth's smooth voice, and Galdran's harsh laughter, echoed with cruel antiphony through my aching skull. I got to my feet. "It's time to go."

Soon we were riding through the chill, wet night air, me in a borrowed hat probably older than I was. Despite the hiss of rain in the trees, we could hear the weird high singing of the Hill Folk's harps, a different sound than any I'd heard yet. The sound seemed to thrum in my bones, and the horses were all skittish.

But we rode steadily, knowing the way despite the minimal light that the moons provided through the rain clouds. Taking little-known paths straight down the mountain, we reached the ridge directly above the fortress well before dawn. There we dismounted, hidden in the ancient trees. The mounts were led away, and the rest of us gathered behind the stones at the edge of the rough cliffs.

Khesot came forward. "We'll go now."

He and his chosen four scouts slipped down through the soggy brush toward the fortress, which was merely a dark bulk below us. The only clear light was on the bridge over the Whitestream, sputtering red torches that cast light on the four sentries walking back and forth.

My eyes stayed on those four half-discernible figures as I wormed my way slowly downhill and took up a position between some rocks, my sword gripped in my hand. A distant portion of my mind was aware of my shivering body; the rain trickling down my scalp into my tunic, which was already heavy with moisture; the tiny noises of the others moving into position around our end of the bridge; and the sound of the tumbling, rushing water below, which drowned the high keening of the Hill Folk harps on the peaks.

A faint movement distracted me as Oria elbow-crawled up to my side. Her profile was outlined by the light from those faraway torches as she looked down on the castle below.

"I'm sorry, Oria," I breathed.

She did not turn her head. "For what?"

"All our plans when we were growing up. All the fine things we'd have had after we won. Making you a duchess—"

She grunted softly. "That was no more than dream-weaving. I don't want to be a duchess. Never did. Well, after my fourteenth year, I didn't. That was you, wanting it for me."

For the first time a flicker of emotion broke briefly through the aching numbness around my heart. "But when we talked..."

She rested her chin on her tightly folded fists, staring down at the castle. I could see tiny reflections of the ruddy torches in her eyes, so steady and unblinking was her gaze. "The only way for me to be a noble is to become a scribe or a herald and work my way up through the government service ranks, and I don't want to write others' things, or to take records, and I don't want to get mixed up with governments—with the kind of people who want to rule over others. Seems like the wrong people get killed, the nice ones. I want..." She sighed and stopped.

"Tell me," I said. "We can dream-weave once more."

"I want to run a house. You can *control* that—make life comfortable, and pleasant, and beautiful. My dream was always that, or partly that..."

Once again she stopped, and this time the gleam of the torches in her eyes was liquid. A quick motion with her finger, a lowering of her long lashes, and the gleam was gone.

"Go on," I said.

She dropped her head down. "You never saw it, Mel. You're just what Mama calls you, a summer flower, a late bloomer."

"I don't understand."

She breathed a laugh. "I know. That's just it! Well, it's all nothing now, so why not admit what a henwit I've been? There's another way to be an aristo, and that's marriage. I never cared about status so much as I did about the idea of marriage. With a specific person."

"Marriage," I repeated, and then a blindingly new idea struck me. "You mean—Branaric?"

She shrugged. "I gave it up three summers ago, when I realized that our living like sisters all our lives meant he saw me as one."

"Oh, Ria." Pain squeezed my heart. "How I wish our lives had gone differently! If Bran were alive—"

"It still wouldn't have happened," she murmured. "And I've

already made my peace with it. That's an old dream. I'm here now because Debegri will do his best to kill our new dreams." She nudged me with her elbow. "Truth is, I rather liked being heart-free last summer, except you didn't notice that, either—you've never tried flirting, much less twoing. You just dance the dances to be dancing, you don't watch the boys watch you when we dance. You don't watch them dance." She chuckled softly. "You don't even peek at the boys' side at the bathhouse."

I reached back in memory, realized how much I had neglected to notice. Not that it had mattered.

My cold lips stretched into a smile. "The boys never looked at me, anyway. Not when they had you to look at."

"Some of that is who you are," she responded. "They never forgot that. But the rest is that you never cared when they did look at you."

And now it's too late. But I didn't say that. Instead, I turned my eyes to those four figures in their steady pacing and let my mind drift back to old memories, summer memories. How much of life had I missed while dedicating myself to Papa's war?

After an uncountable interval a voice murmured on my other side, "It's taking a long time." It was Jusar, our trained soldier. "Worries me."

With a jolt, I remembered Khesot and his party. Back to the war, and my losses. I steeled myself: no more dream drifting. "We'll watch the sentries, see if anyone comes out from the castle with a message for them," I whispered back. "That would mean trouble. Otherwise, as soon as we have light enough, we attack. Khesot or no."

He nodded. In the faint light from those torches below, I saw him swallow, then compress his lips, as though forming a resolve.

I returned to my vigil. The darkness seemed to endure forever, outside of me, inside. Now I wanted only to move, to run, to strike against a pair of watchful gray eyes and extinguish the light of laughter I saw there. And then be swallowed whole by the darkness, forever ...

"Dawn."

I had dropped into another, darker reverie without knowing; Oria's soft voice broke it. I lifted my head, saw the faint bluish light just barely distinguishing one tree from another. It touched the fortress, giving the flat bulk the dimension of depth, of height; and as I watched, the massive stones of the walls took on texture. From the peaks there was silence.

Now that action was nigh, I felt a strange calm settle over me, blanketing me from emotion, from thought, even. Instinct would guide me. It remained only to give the signal, and emerge from our cover, and attack.

I gripped my sword tighter and rose to my knees, bracing myself. Once I raised my arm, there would be no turning back.

A deep *graunch*ing noise, the protest of old metal, came from the fortress, and I froze, waiting. My heart racketed in my chest as I peered down through the early-morning gloom.

Slowly the big gates opened. Red-gold fire glow from inside silhouetted a number of figures who moved out toward the bridge, where the strengthening light picked out the drawn swords, the spears, the dark cloaks, and the helmed heads of the Renselaeus warriors. They were wearing their own colors, and battle gear. No liveries, no pretense of being mere servants. In the center of their formation were Khesot and the four others—unarmed.

There were no shouts, no trumpets, nothing but the ringing of iron-shod boots on the stones of the bridge, and the clank of ready weaponry.

Could we rescue them? I could not see Khesot's face, but in the utter stillness with which they stood, I read hopelessness.

I readied myself once again—

Then from the center of their forces stepped a single equerry, with a white scarf tied to a pole. He started up the path that we meant to descend. As he walked the light strengthened, now illuminating details. Still with that weird detachment I looked at his curly hair, the freckles on his face, his small nose. *We could cut him down in moments*, I thought, and then winced the thought away. We were not Galdran. I waited.

He stopped not twenty-five paces from me and said loudly, "Countess, we request a parley."

Which made it obvious they knew we were there.

Questions skittered through my mind. Had Khesot talked? How otherwise could the enemy have seen us? The only noise now was the rain, pattering softly with the magnificent indifference of nature for the tangled passions of humans.

I stood up. "Here. State your message."

"A choice. You surrender, and your people can then disperse to their homes. Otherwise, we start with them." He pointed to the bridge. "Then everyone else." He lifted his hand, indicating the ridge up behind us.

I turned, and shock burned through me when I saw an uncountable host lined along the rocks we'd descended from half a night ago.

They had us boxed.

Which meant that we had walked right into a waiting trap.

I looked down at the bridge again. Through the curtain of rain the figures were clearer now. Khesot, in the center, stood next to a tall slim man with pale yellow hair.

I closed my eyes, fought for control, then opened my eyes again. "Everyone goes to their homes? Including Khesot and the four down there?"

"Everyone," the boy said flatly, "except you, Countess."

Which meant I was staking my life against everyone else's. And of course there was no answer but one to be made to that.

With black murder in my heart, I flung my sword down rather than hand it over. Stepping across it, I walked past the equerry, whose footfalls I then heard crunching behind me.

Wild vows of death and destruction flowed through my mind

as I walked down the trail. No one moved. Only the incessant rain came down, a silver veil, as I slipped down the pathway, then reached the bridge, then crossed it, stalking angrily between the lines of waiting warriors.

When I neared the other end of the bridge, the Marquis turned his back and walked inside the fortress, and the others followed, Khesot and the four scouts still some distance from me. I could not see their faces, could not speak to them.

I walked through the big gates, which closed. Across the courtyard the south gates stood open, and before them mounted warriors waited.

With them were two saddled, riderless horses, one a familiar gray.

In silence the entourage moved toward them, and the Marquis mounted the gray, who sidled nervously, newly shod hooves ringing on the stones.

Khesot and the others were now behind me, invisible behind the crowd of warriors in Renselaeus colors, all of whom watched and waited in silence.

It was weird, dreamlike, the only reality the burning rage in my heart.

Someone motioned me toward the single riderless horse, and I climbed up. For a moment the ground seemed to heave under the animal's feet, but I shook my head and the world righted itself, and I glared through the softly falling rain to the cold gray gaze of the Marquis of Shevraeth, heir to Renselaeus.

His horse danced a few steps. He looked over his shoulder at me, the low brim of his hat now hiding his eyes.

"Ride," he said.

TWENTY

No one else spoke.

Surrounded by warriors but utterly isolated, I rode at a gallop through the quiet rain as daylight strengthened all around me. Birds squawked warnings, and once a deer crashed through a shrub and bounded with breathtaking grace across the road in front of us. Humans and horses stayed on their path, racing headlong.

I don't know how long we rode. At the time, the trip seemed endless; looking back, it was curiously short. Memory warps time, as it does the sights and sounds and smells of reality; for what shapes it is emotion, which can twist what seems clear, just as the surface of a pond seems to bend the stick thrust into the water.

I know only that we were still deep in the Old Forest, which meant a ride to the south, when at some point we left the road, and then the trails, and at last came to a clearing sheltered by ancient trees, in which stood a very old, mossy-stoned wood gatherer's cottage.

The riders fanned out, but my immediate escort rode straight to the overhanging rusty roof that formed a rudimentary barn. The Marquis dismounted and stretched out his hand to grip the bridle of my horse.

"Inside," he said to me.

I dismounted. Again the ground seemed to heave beneath my feet, but I leaned against the shoulders of my mount until the world steadied, and then I straightened up.

The Marquis walked toward the open doorway.

In a kind of blank daze, I followed the sweeping black cloak inside and down a tiny hall, to a door made of old, rickety twigs bound together. The Marquis opened this and waved me into a little room. I took two steps inside it, looked—

And there, lying on a narrow bed, with books and papers strewn about him, was my brother, Branaric.

"Mel!" he exclaimed. "Burn it, you were right," he said past me. "Ran her to ground at Vesingrui, eh?"

A voice spoke behind me: "They were just about to drop on us."

I turned, saw the Marquis leaning in the doorway, a growing puddle of rainwater at his feet.

For a long moment I could do nothing except stand as if rooted. The world seemed about to dissolve for a sickening moment, but I sucked in a ragged breath and it righted again, and I threw myself down on my knees next to the bed, knocking my soggy, shapeless hat off, and hugged Branaric fiercely.

"Mel, Mel," Bran said, laughing, then he groaned and fell back on his pillows. "Softly, girl. Curse it! I'm weak as a newborn kitten."

"And will be for a time," came the voice from the doorway. "Once your explanations have been made, I exhort you to remember Mistress Kylar's warning."

"Aye, I've it well in mind," Bran said. And as the door closed, he looked up at me from fever-bright eyes. "He was right! Said you'd go straight after 'em, sword and knife. What's with you?"

"You said, 'A trap.' I thought it was *them*," I muttered through suddenly numb lips. "Wasn't it?"

"Didn't you see the riding of greeners?" Bran retorted. "It was Debegri, right enough. He had paid informants in those inns, for he was on the watch for your return. Why d'you think Vidanric sent the escort?"

"Vidanric?"

"His name," Branaric said, still staring at me with that odd gaze. "You could try to use it—only polite. After all, Shevraeth is just a title, and he doesn't go about calling either of us Tlanth."

I'd rather cut out my tongue, I thought, but I said nothing.

"Anyway—life, sister—if he'd wanted me dead, why not in the comfort of his own home, where he could do a better job?"

I shook my head. "It made sense to me."

"It makes sense when you have a castle-sized grudge." He sighed. "It was the Renselaeus escort, hard on their heels, that attacked Debegri's gang and saved my life. Our friend the Marquis wasn't far behind—he'd just found out about the spies, he said. Between us we pieced together what happened, and what I said, and what you'd likely do. I thought you'd stay home. He said you'd ride back down the mountain breathing fire and hunting his blood. He was right." He started to laugh, but it came out a groan, and he closed his eyes for a long breath. Then, "Arrow clipped me on the right, or I'd be finished. But I can't talk long—I'm already feeling sick. Galdran is just behind Debegri. He's coming up to make an example of Tlanth himself. Talk all over the countryside..." He stopped, taking several slow breaths, then he squinted at me. "Ask Vidanric. He's the one explained it to me."

"First tell me, are we prisoners, or not?"

"No," Bran said. "But mark my words: The end is nigh. And we're either for Renselaeus or for Galdran."

"You mean Shevraeth is coming into the open?"

"Yes."

"Then—he's going to face the whole army?"

Bran breathed deeply again. "Galdran has very few friends," he murmured, then closed his eyes. "Go change. Eat."

I nodded, the numbness spreading from my lips to my brain, and to my heart. "Get your rest. We'll talk when you feel better."

I walked out, and closed the door, and leaned against it, my forehead grinding against the rough wood.

Finally I forced myself to look up, to move. A sudden, terrible weariness had settled over me. I saw an open door at the other end of the little hall, and yellow light pouring from it.

The light drew me more than anything. Straightening up, I crossed the hall. Inside the room Shevraeth sat at a rough stone table near a fireplace, in which a crackling fire roared. At one end of the table was spread a map, at the other a tray of food, as yet untouched. Against an adjacent wall was a narrow bed, with more papers and another map spread over its neatly smoothed blanket. Three or four warriors in the familiar livery sat on mats around the table, all talking in quiet voices, but when the Marquis saw me, they fell silent and rose to their feet.

In silence, they filed past me, and I was left alone with the person who, the day before, I'd wanted to kill even more than Galdran Merindar.

"Take a swig." Shevraeth held out a flagon. "You're going to need it, I'm afraid."

I crossed the room, sank cross-legged onto the nearest mat. With one numb hand I took the flagon, squeezed a share of its contents into my mouth; and gasped as the fire of distilled bristic burned its way inside me. I took a second sip and with stinging eyes handed the flagon back.

"Blue lips," he said, with that faint smile. "You're going to have a whopping cold."

I looked up at the color burning along his cheekbones, and the faint lines of strain in his forehead, and made a discovery. "So are you," I said. "Hah!" I added, obscurely pleased.

His mouth quirked. "Do you have any questions?"

"Yes." My voice came out hoarse, and I cleared my throat. "Bran said Galdran is coming after us. Why? I thought it had been made abundantly clear that—thanks to you—we were defeated, and that was after he'd already decided we were of no account."

"Here. Eat something." He pulled the tray over and pointed to the bread-and-cheese on it, and at the half of some kind of fruit tart.

I picked up the bread and bit into it as he said, "But his cousin did not encompass your defeat, despite the fact that you were outnumbered and outmaneuvered. This is the more galling for Galdran, you must understand, when you consider the enormous loss of prestige he has suffered of late."

"Loss of prestige? In what way?" I asked.

He sat back, his eyes glinting with amusement. "First there was the matter of a—very—public announcement of a pending execution, following which the intended victim escapes. Then . . . didn't you stop to consider that the countryside folk who endured many long days of constant martial interference in the form of searches, curfews, and threats might have a few questions about the justice of said threats—or the efficacy of all these armed and mounted soldiery tramping through their fields and farms unsuccessfully trying to flush a single unarmed, rather unprepossessing individual? Especially when said individual took great care not to endanger anyone beyond the first—anonymous—family to give her succor, to whom she promised there would be no civil war?"

I gasped. "I never promised that. How could I? I promised that Bran and I wouldn't carry our fight into their territory."

Shevraeth's smile was wry. "But you must know how gossip gets distorted when it burns across the countryside, faster than a summer hayfire. And you had given the word of a countess. You have to remember that a good part of our . . . influence . . . is vouchsafed in our status, after the manner of centuries of habit. It is a strength and a weakness, a good and an evil."

I winced, thinking of Ara, who knew more about history than I did.

"Though you seem to be completely unaware of it, you have become a heroine to the entire kingdom. What is probably more important to you is that your cause is now on everyone's lips, even if—so far—it's only being whispered about. With the best will in the world, Galdran's spies could only find out what was being said, but not by whom. Imagine, if you can, the effect."

I tried. Too tired to actually think of much beyond when I might lay my head down, and where, I looked across the room at that bed—then away quickly—and said as stoutly as I could, "I hope it skewered him good."

"He's angry enough to be on his way to face us, but we shall discuss it later. Permit me to suggest that you avail yourself of the room next to your brother's, which was hastily excavated last night. We'll be using this place as our command post for the next day or so."

I wavered to my feet, swayed, leaned against the wall. "Yes. Well." I tried to think of something appropriate to say, but nothing came to mind.

So I walked out and found my way to the room, unlatched the door. A tiny corner hearth radiated a friendly heat from a fire. A fire—they used a Fire Stick just for me. Was there a family somewhere doing without? Or did the Hill Folk know—somehow—of the Marquis's cause, and had they tendered their approval by giving his people extras? I shook my head, beyond comprehending anything. Near the fireplace was a campbed, nicely set up, with a bedroll all stretched out and waiting, and a folded cloak for a pillow.

Somehow I got my muddy, soggy clothes off and slid the wallet with Debegri's letter under the folded-cloak pillow. Then I climbed into that bed, and I don't remember putting my head down.

It was dark when I woke; I realized I'd heard the door click shut.

Turning my head, I looked into the leaping fire, saw lying on a stool in front of it—getting warm—some clothes. Next to the stool was an ewer with steaming water, a cloth, and a comb.

I could have lain there much longer, but I took this as a hint that I ought to get up, and when I remembered Bran lying in the next room, it was easier to motivate myself.

It did take effort, though. My skin hurt and my head ached,

sure signs that I was indeed coming down with some illness. I cleaned up as best as I could, combed out my rain-washed hair, and put on the familiar oversized Renselaeus livery donated by some anonymous person not even remotely my size. Again I stashed the letter inside the tunic, then I left the room.

I found the other two in Bran's room, and one look at their faces made it abundantly clear that they felt no better than I did. Not that the Marquis had a red nose or a thick voice—he even looked aristocratic when sick, I thought with disgust. But Bran sneezed frequently, and from the pungent smell of bristic in the air, he had had recourse to the flagon.

"Mel!" he exclaimed when I opened the door. And he laughed. "Look at you! You're drowning in that kit." He turned his head to address Shevraeth. "Ain't anyone undersized among your people?"

"Obviously not," I said tartly, and helped myself to the flagon that I saw on the bed. A swig of bristic did help somewhat. "Unless the sight of me is intended to provide some cheap amusement for the warriors."

"Well, I won't come off much better," Bran said cheerily.

"That I resent," the Marquis said with his customary drawl. "Seeing as it is my wardrobe that is gracing your frame."

Branaric only laughed, then he said, "Now that we're all together, and I'm still sober, what's the word?"

"The latest report is that the King is a day or two's march from here, well ensconced in the midst of his army. Debegri is with him, and it seems there have been some disagreements on the manner in which you two are to be dealt with. Galdran wants to lay Tlanth to waste, but Debegri, of course, has his eye to a title and land at last."

Bran rubbed his chin. "Only one of that family not landed, right?"

"To the Baron's festering annoyance. Despite their pose of eternal brotherhood, they have never really liked—or trusted—one another. It has suited Galdran well to have Nenthar Debegri serve as his watch-beast, for Debegri has been scrupulous about enforcing

Galdran's laws. Enthusiastic, I should say. If he cannot have land, Debegri's preference is to ride the countryside acting the bully. It has made him unpopular, which does Galdran no harm."

"So what's the plan?"

"I believe that our best plan is to flush them out. If we can capture them both, there will be little reason for the others to fight."

"But if they're in the midst of the army—" Bran started.

"Bait," I said, seeing the plan at once. "There has to be bait to bring them to the front." Thinking rapidly, I added, "And I know who's to be the bait. Us, right? Only, how to get them to meet us?"

"The letter," Branaric said. "They know now that we have it."

Both looked at me, but I said nothing.

"Even if we don't have it," the Marquis said easily, "it's enough to say we do to get them to meet us. If they break the truce or try anything untoward, a chosen group will grab them, and my warriors will disperse in all directions and reassemble at a certain place on my border a week later, at which time we will reassess. I can give you all the details of the plan if you wish them."

Bran snorted a laugh. "I'm in. As if we had a choice!"

"*Do* we have a choice?" I asked, instantly hostile.

"I am endeavoring to give you the semblance of one," Shevraeth replied in his most polite voice.

"And if we don't agree?" I demanded.

"Then you will remain here in safety until events are resolved."

"So we *are* prisoners, then."

Bran was chuckling and wiping his eyes. "Life, sister, how you remind me of that old spaniel of Khesot's, Skater, when he thought someone was going to pinch his favorite chew-stick. Remember him?"

"Bran—" I began, now thoroughly exasperated.

"Well, it isn't the goals, Mel, for we've the same ones, in essentials. It's you being stubborn, just like old Skater. Admit it!"

"I admit only that I don't trust *him* as far as I can throw a horse," I fumed. "We're still prisoners, and you just sit there and laugh! Well, go ahead. I think I'll go back to sleep. The company is better." And I stalked to the door, went out, and slammed it.

Of course I could still hear Bran wheezing with laughter. The ancient doors were not of tapestry but of wood, extremely flimsy and ill-fitted wood, serving no real purpose beyond blocking the room from sight. Tapestry manners required I move away at once, but I hesitated until I heard Bran say, "She won't rat out on us. Let me talk to her, and she'll see reason."

"I'd give her some time before you attempt it," came the wry answer.

"She usually doesn't stay mad long," Bran said carelessly.

Again habit urged me to move. I knew to stay made me a spy-ears, which no one over the age of four is excused in being, yet I didn't move. I *couldn't* move. So I stood there and listened—and thus proved the old proverb about eavesdroppers getting what they deserve.

Shevraeth said, "I'm very much afraid it's my fault. We met under the worst of circumstances, and we seem to have misunderstood one another to a lethal degree."

Bran said, "No, if it's anyone's fault, it's ours—my parents' and mine. You have to realize our mother saw Tlanth as a haven from her Court life. All she had to do was potter around her garden and play her harp. I don't think Mel even knows Mother spent a few years at Erev-li-Erval, learning Kheras in the Court of the Empress. Mel scarcely talked before she started hearing stories on the immoral, rotten, lying Court decorations. Mama liked seeing her running wild with Oria and the village brats. Then Mama was killed, and Papa mostly lived shut in his tower, brooding over the past. He didn't seem to know what to do with Mel. She couldn't read or write, wouldn't even sit still indoors—all summer she would disappear for a week at a time, roaming in the hills. I think she knows more about the ways of the Hill Folk than she does about what actually happens at Court. Anyhow, I taught her her letters just a year or so ago, mostly as an excuse to get away from my books. She liked it well enough, except there isn't much to read up there anymore, beyond what Papa thought I ought to know for preparing a war."

"I see. Yet you've told me she shared in the command of your rebels."

Bran laughed again. "That's because after she learned to read, Mel learned figuring, on her own, and took it over."

"You mean, she took charge of your business affairs?"

"Such as they were, yes. Taxes, all that. It's why I told her she had half the title. *Life!* She could've had the title, and the leadership, for all of me, except we promised Papa when he died that we'd go it together. And working toward the war—it was easier when we did it together. She turned it into a game, though I think she saw it as real before I did." He sighed. "Well, I know she did. Curst traps prove it."

"Your family was reputed to have a good library."

"Until Papa burned it, after Mama died. Everything gone, and neither of us knowing what we'd lost. Or, I knew and didn't care, but Mel didn't even know. Curse it, her maid is sister to the blacksmith. Julen's never been paid, but sees to Mel because she's sorry for her."

"There has been, I take it, little contact with family, then?"

"Papa had no family left in this part of the world. As for Mama's royal cousins, when they moved north to Cheras al Kherval, my parents lost touch, and I never did see any reason to try..."

I slipped away then, raging against my brother and the Marquis, against Julen for pitying me when I'd thought she was my friend, against nosy listeners such as myself...against Papa, and Galdran, and war, and Galdran again, against the Empress and every courtier ever born.

I sat in the room they'd given me and glared into the roaring fire, angry with the entire universe.

191

TWENTY-ONE

BUT AFTER A TIME EVEN MY TEMPER TANTRUMS HAVE to give way to rational thought, and I faced at last what ought to have been obvious from the very beginning: We'd lost because we were ignorant. And of the two of us, I was the worse off, because I hadn't even known I was ignorant.

An equerry tapped at the door and announced that supper was being served.

I sat where I was and waged a short fierce inner battle. Either I could sit and sulk—in which case they would want to know why—or I could go out there, pretend nothing was amiss, and do what needed doing.

The table in the Marquis's room was set for the three of us. I sniffed the air, which was pleasant with the summer-grass smell of brewing listerblossom. Somehow this eased my sore spirits just a little. I knelt down next to my brother, whose bed pillows cushioned him, and poured myself some of the tea. It felt good on my raw throat.

For a time I just sat there with my eyes closed, sipping occasionally, while the other two continued a conversation about the difficulties of supply procurement that they had obviously begun before I returned. At first I listened to the voices: Bran's husky, slow, with laughter in it as a constant and pleasant undercurrent, and Shevraeth's soft, emotionless, with words drawn out in a court drawl to give them emphasis, rather than using changes in tone or timbre. The complexity of Shevraeth's reaction was thus masked, which—I realized—was more irritating to me than his voice, which didn't precisely grate on the ears. It was an advantage that I had no access to; I seemed to be incapable of hiding my reactions.

The tea restored to me enough presence of mind to bring the sense of their words, instead of mere sound. They were still discoursing on supply sources and how to protect supply lines, and Bran kept looking to me for corroboration, for in truth, I knew more about this than he did. Then I realized that it was an unexceptionable subject introduced so that I might take part; but I saw in that a gesture of pity, and my black mood threatened to descend again.

Then came the food—roasted fowl, with vegetables mixed into a sauce made from the meat drippings, and a hot tart made with apples and spices and wine, by the smell. My appetite woke up suddenly, and for a time all I had attention for was my plate.

The others conversed little, and at the end of the meal I looked up, saw the unmistakable marks of fever in their faces. Branaric grinned. "What a trio we make! Look at us."

Annoyance flared anew. Glaring at him, I said hoarsely, "Look at yourself. I'd rather spare myself the nightmare, which would affright even a half-sighted gargoyle."

Bran gaped at me in surprise, then laughed. "Just keep that temper sharp. You'll need it, for we may be on the march tomorrow."

"Oh, good," I croaked with as much enthusiasm as I could muster.

It sounded about as false as it felt, and Bran laughed again; but before he could say anything, the Marquis suggested that we all retire, for the morrow promised to be a long day.

———

"Curse it," Bran said the next morning, standing before the fire in shirt and trousers with his shoulder stiffly bandaged. "You think this necessary?"

He pointed at the mail coats lying on the table, their linked steel rings gleaming coldly in the light of two glowglobes. It was well before dawn. The Marquis had woken us himself, with the news that Galdran's forces were nigh. And his messengers had brought from Renselaeus the mail coats, newly made and expensive.

"Treachery—" Shevraeth paused to cough and to catch his breath. He, too, stood there in only shirt and trousers and boots, and I looked away quickly, embarrassed. "We should be prepared for treachery. It was his idea to send archers against you in the mountains. He will have them with him now." He coughed again, the rattling cough of a heavy cold.

I sighed. My own fever and aches had all settled into my throat, and my voice was gone.

Bran was the worst off. Besides the wound in his shoulder, he coughed, sneezed, and sounded hoarse. His eyes and nose watered constantly. Luckily the Renselaeus munificence extended to a besorceled handkerchief that stayed dry and clean despite its heavy use.

Groaning and wincing, Bran lifted his arm just high enough for a couple of equerries to slip the chain mail over his head. As it settled onto him, *ching*ing softly, he winced and said, "Feels like I've got a horse lying athwart my shoulders."

I picked up the one set aside for me and retreated to my room to put it on, and then the tunic they'd given me. Branaric's wallet containing Debegri's letter lay safe and snug in my waistband.

When I came back, Branaric started laughing. "A mouse in mail!" he said, pointing. He and Shevraeth both had battle tunics on, and swords belted at their sides; they looked formidable, whereas I felt I looked ridiculous. My mail shirt was the smallest of the three, but it was still much too large, and it bunched and folded beneath my already outsized tunic, making me feel like an overstuffed cushion.

But the Marquis said nothing at all as he indicated a table where a choice of weapons lay, with belts and baldrics of various sizes and styles. In silence I belted on a short sword similar to the one I'd thrown down in surrender above the Vesingrui fortress. I found a helm that fit pretty well over my braid coronet, and then I was ready.

Within a short time we were mounted on fresh chargers that were also armored. Despite the chill outside I started warm, for we'd each drunk an infusion of listerblossoms against illness.

Our way was lit by torches as we raced over the ancient road, under trees that had been old before my family first came to Tlanth. Except for the rhythm of hooves there was no sound, but I sensed that forest life was watching us.

According to the plan two equerries were sent on ahead. The rest of us rode steadily as dawn started to lift the heavy shroud of darkness. A fine rain still fell, and the trees dripped on us, spattering our faces with cold water. Strong was the green smell of wet loam and forest. I breathed deeply of it, finding it comforting in an odd way. No one talked much, but I kept thinking about the fact that we were riding deliberately into danger—that Galdran would see treachery as expedience. Our plan depended on the Renselaeus warriors being fast and accurate and brave, for they were as outnumbered as Bran and I had been up in the mountains.

I was also, therefore, intensely aware that my life was now in the hands of people I had considered enemies not two dawns ago. Did they still consider me one?

I tried to calm my nerves by laughing at myself; for someone who so recently had tried her best to ride to her death, my innards were a pit of snakes, and my palms were sweaty despite the rain. Bran was alive, I was alive, and suddenly I wanted to stay that way. I wanted to go home and clean out the castle and replant Mama's garden. I wanted to see Oria and Julen and Khesot again, and I wanted to walk on the high peaks and dance with the Hill Folk on long summer nights, miming age-old stories to the windborne music...

I blinked. Had I just heard a reed pipe?

I lifted my head and listened, heard nothing but the thud of hooves and clatter of our accoutrements, and the soft rain in the leaves overhead.

At last the equerries returned—safe, I guessed, only because of Galdran's curiosity and his desire to get his bejeweled fingers around our throats.

"They're on the plain below the last hill, Your Grace," said one, pointing backward. "The King says he will meet you at the bridge over the Thereas River."

"Cover?" Shevraeth said, and coughed.

As if in sympathy Bran sneezed, and despite the danger, I felt a weird impulse to laugh. *If we win, will our colds be in the songs?*

"Thick, Your Grace. Trees, shrubbery. Both sides."

"Right. Then we can expect archers behind every bush, and swords waiting in the trees. Be ready for anything," he said, waving them on.

They raced off to spread the word.

"Well," Bran said, wincing as our horses moved forward again, "you wanted them in the forest."

"Equal things out a little," was the reply, still in the cool drawl. "Ready, Lady Meliara?"

"Let's get it over with," I croaked.

The Marquis gave me that assessing look, then turned to Bran. "Ready for a ride?"

"Certainly," my brother said, though without any of his usual humor.

Shevraeth reached into his saddlebag and pulled out the flagon. Wordlessly he passed it to Bran, who took a couple swigs, then, gasping, passed it to me. I helped myself, and with tearing eyes returned it. The Marquis tipped back his head, took a good slug, then stored it again, and we were off.

There's no use in talking about the plan, because of course nothing went the way it was supposed to. Even the passage of time was horribly distorted. At first the ride to the hill seemed endless, with me sneaking looks at my brother, who was increasingly unsteady in his saddle.

The Marquis insisted on riding in front of us the last little distance, where we saw a row of four horse riders waiting—the outer two bearing banners, dripping from the rain, but the flags' green and gold still brilliant, and the inner two riders brawny and cruel faced and very much at ease, wearing the plumed helms of command.

"I just wanted to see if you traitors would dare to face me," Galdran said, his caustic voice making me feel sick inside. Sick—and angry.

The Marquis bowed low over his horse's withers, every line of his body indicative of irony.

Galdran's face flushed dark purple.

"I confess," Shevraeth drawled, "we had a small wager on whether you would have the courage to face us."

"Kill them!" Galdran roared.

And that's the moment when time changed and everything happened at once. At the edge of my vision I saw arrows fly, but none reached us. A weird humming vibrated through my skull; at first I thought it was just me, then I realized all the war horses, despite their training, were in a panic. For a few short, desperate breaths, all my attention was spent calming my own mount.

Galdran's reared, and he shouted orders at his equerries as he fought to keep his seat. The two banner-bearing warriors flipped up the ends of their poles, flicked away some kind of binding, and aimed sharp steel points at the Marquis as they charged. All around me was chaos—the hiss and clang of steel weapons being drawn, the nickering of horses, grunts and shouts and yells.

"To me! To me!" That was Bran's cry.

Four Renselaeus warriors came to his aid. I kneed my mount forward and brandished my weapon, trying to edge up on Bran's weak side. Horseback fighting was something we'd drilled in rarely, for this was not mountain-type warfare. I met the blade of one of Bran's attackers, and shock rang up my arm. Thoughts chased through my brain; except for those few days with Nessaren's riding, I hadn't practiced for weeks, and now I was going to feel it.

Wondering how I would make it through a hand-to-hand duel, I glanced around—and just then I saw one of Galdran's equerries fall from his saddle, his banner-spear spinning through the air toward me. Instinctively my free hand reached up and I caught the spear by the shaft. Ignoring the sting in my hand, I jammed my sword into its sheath and started whirling the spear round and round, making the banner snap and stream as my prancing, sidling horse circled round my brother. Horses turned their heads and backed away; no one was able to edge up and get in a good blow at Bran, who swayed in his saddle, his bad arm hanging limp. The warriors fell back, and no one swung at me.

Dimly I became aware of an ugly, harsh voice shouting over the crash and thuds of battle. Keeping the banner whirling, I guided my horse with my knees and risked a glance back over my shoulder—and looked straight into Galdran's rage-darkened face. He said something, spittle flying from his mouth, as he pointed straight at me.

A moment later a flicker of movement on my immediate left caused me to glance round. Shevraeth was there, next to me. "Fall back," he ordered, his voice sharp.

"No. Got to protect Bran—"

There was no time for more. The Marquis was beset by furious attackers as the King shouted orders from a short distance away. Then more riders appeared from somewhere, and for a moment everything was too chaotic to follow. I found myself suddenly on the edge of the battle; there were too many fighters on both sides between my brother and me. Too many fighters in the liveries of the Baron and the King. Despair burned through me, cold as winter ice.

We were losing.

Then my horse plunged aside, I shifted in the saddle, and I found myself face-to-face with Galdran. He glared at me with hatred; I had this sudden, strange feeling that if we had both been small children facing each other in a village squabble he would have screamed at me, *It's all your fault!*

His lips drew back from his teeth. "You, I will kill myself," he snarled, and he raised his great, flat-bladed sword.

I cast away the flimsy spear and drew my sword just a scarce moment before Galdran struck. The first blow nearly knocked me out off the horse. I parried it—just barely—pain shooting up my arm into my back. My arm was numb, so I used both hands to raise my blade against the expected next blow.

But as Galdran's sword came down toward my head, it was met by a ringing strike that sent sparks arcing through the air. I looked—saw the Marquis, hair flying, horse dancing, circling round Galdran and forcing his attention away. Then the two were fighting desperately, the King falling back. I watched in fascination until two of the King's guards rode to Galdran's aid, and Shevraeth was suddenly fighting against three.

It seemed that the Marquis was going to lose, and I realized I couldn't watch. Remembering my brother, I forced my mount round so I could ride to his aid. But when I spotted him in the chaos of lunging horses and crashing weapons, he was staring past my shoulder, his eyes distended.

"Meliara!" he yelled, trying to ride toward me.

I turned my head, saw the Marquis now fighting against three guards; and once again the King was coming directly at me, sword swinging in a blur. I flung my sword at him and ducked. A blow caught me painfully across the back of my helm, and darkness rushed up to swallow me.

TWENTY-TWO

I WOKE RELUCTANTLY, FOR MY HEAD ACHED LIKE A stone mountain had fallen on it. I sat up, ignoring the crashing in my skull, and swung my legs over the edge of my cot. I was back in the wood gatherer's cottage.

The fire was leaping, the room warm. I glanced at the window, saw light outside. As I stood I realized the chain mail was gone, as was the tunic. All I had on were the shirt and trousers I'd been wearing, wrinkled but dry. The wallet with Debegri's letter was still tucked safely in my waistband.

I looked around for the tunic so I could leave the room; not for worlds would I go out dressed thus into the midst of a lot of staring Renselaeus warriors.

Unless Galdran has won! The terrible thought froze me for a moment, but then I looked down at that fire and realized that if Galdran had beaten us, I'd hardly be in such comfortable surroundings again. More likely I'd have woken in some dungeon somewhere, with clanking chains attached to every limb.

I held my head in my hands, trying to get the strength to stand; then my door opened, thrust by an impatient hand. Branaric stood there, grinning in surprise.

"You're awake! Healer said you'd likely sleep out the day."

I nodded slowly, eyeing his flushed cheeks and overbright eyes. His right arm rested in a sling. "You are also sick," I observed.

"Merrily so," he agreed, "but I cannot for the life of me keep still. Burn it! Truth to tell, I never thought I'd live to see this day."

"What day?" I asked, and then, narrowly, "We're not prisoners, are we? Where is Galdran?"

"Ash," Bran said with a laugh.

I gaped. "Dead?"

"Dead and burned, though no one shed a tear at his funeral fire. And you should have seen his minions scatter beforehand! The rest couldn't surrender fast enough!" He laughed again, then, "Ulp! Forgot. Want tea?"

"Oh yes," I said with enthusiasm. "I was just looking for my tunic. Or rather, the one I was wearing."

"Mud," he said succinctly. "Galdran smacked you off your horse and you landed flat in a mud puddle. Hold there!"

I sat down on the bunk again, questions swarming through my mind like angry bees.

Branaric was back in a moment, carefully carrying a brimming mug in his one good hand, and some folded cloth and a plain brown citizen's hat tucked under his arm. "Here ye are, sister," he said cheerily. "Let's celebrate."

I took the mug, and as he toasted me with a pretend one, I lifted mine to him and drank deeply. The listerblossom infusion flooded me from head to heels with soothing warmth. I sighed with relief, then said, "Now, tell me everything."

He chuckled and leaned against the door. "That's a comprehensive command! Where to begin?"

"With Galdran. How did he die?"

"Vidanric. Sword," Bran said, waving his index finger in a parry-and-thrust. "Just after Galdran tried to brain you from the back. Neatest work I've ever seen. He promised to introduce me to his old sword master when we get to Athanarel."

" 'We'? You and the Marquis?"

"We can discuss it when we meet for supper, soon's he gets back. Life! I don't think he's sat down since we returned yestereve. I'm tied here by the heels, healer's orders, but there'll be enough for us all to do soon."

I opened my mouth to say that I did not want to go to Athanarel, but I could almost hear his rallying tone—and the fact, bitterly faced but true, that part of my image as the ignorant little sister guaranteed that Bran seldom took me seriously. So I shook my head instead. "Tell me more."

"Well, that's the main of it, in truth. They were all pretty disgusted—both sides, I think—when Galdran went after you. He didn't even have the courage to face me, and I was weavin' on my horse like a one-legged rooster. One o' his bully boys knocked me clean out of the saddle just after Galdran hit you. Anyway, Vidanric went after the King, quick and cool as ice, and the others went after Debegri—but he nearly got away. I say 'nearly' because it was one of his own people got him squarely in the back with an arrow—what's more, that one didn't sprout. Now, if that ain't justice, I don't know what is!" He touched his shoulder.

"What? Arrow? Sprout? Was that somehow related to that strange humming just as everything started—or did I imagine that?"

"Not unless we all did." Bran looked sober for a moment. "Magic. The Hill Folk were right there, watching and spell casting! First time I ever heard of them interfering in one of our human brangles, but they did. Those arrows from Galdran's archers all sprouted leaves soon's they left the bow, and they fell to the ground, and curse me if they didn't start takin' root. Soon's the archers saw that, they threw away their bows and panicked. Weirdest thing I ever saw. That hilltop will be all forest by winter, or I'm a lapdog."

"Whoosh," I said, sitting down.

He then remembered the cloth under his arm and tossed it into my lap.

I held up yet another tunic that was shapeless and outsized, but I was glad to see it was plain, thick, and well made.

"Found that in someone's kit. Knew you hated wearing these." Bran indicated his own tunic, another of the Renselaeus ones.

Thinking of appearing yet again as a ridiculous figure in ill-fitting, borrowed clothing, I tried to summon a smile. "Thanks."

He touched his shoulder with tentative fingers, then winced. "I'll lie down until Vidanric gets back. Then, mind, we're all to plan together, and soon's we're done here, we ride for Athanarel—all three of us."

"Why all three of us?"

"There's work that needs doing," Branaric said, serious again.

"What can I possibly do besides serve as a figure of fun for the Court to laugh at again? I don't *know* anything—besides how to lose a war; and I don't think anyone is requiring that particular bit of knowledge." I tried to sound reasonable, but even I could hear the bitterness in my own voice.

My brother sighed. "I don't know what I'll do, either, except I'll put my hand to anything I'm asked. That's what our planning session is to be about, soon's they return. So save your questions for then, and I don't want any more of this talk of prisoners and grudges and suchlike. Vidanric saved your life—he's been a true ally, can't you see it now?"

"He saved it twice," I corrected without thinking.

"He what?" My brother straightened up.

"In Chovilun dungeon. Didn't I tell you?" Then I remembered I hadn't gotten that far before Debegri's trap had closed about us.

Bran pursed his lips, staring at me with an uncharacteristic expression. "Interesting. I didn't know that."

"Well, you got in the way of an arrow before I got a chance to finish the story," I explained.

"Except, Vidanric didn't tell me, either." Branaric opened his mouth, hesitated, then shook his head. "Well, it seems we all have some talking to do. I'm going to lie down first. You drink your tea." He went out, and I heard the door to his room shut and his cot creak.

I looked away, staring at the merry fire, my thoughts ranging back over the headlong pace of the recent days. Suddenly I knew that Shevraeth had recognized me outside that town, and I knew why he hadn't done anything about it: because Debegri was with him then. The Marquis and his people had searched day and night in order to find me before Debegri did—searched not to kill me, but in order to save me from certain death at Debegri's hands.

Why hadn't he told me? Because I'd called him a liar and untrustworthy, and had made it plain I wasn't going to change my opinion, no matter what. Then why hadn't he told my brother, who did trust him?

That I couldn't answer. And in a sense it didn't matter. What did matter was that I had been wrong about Shevraeth. I had been so wrong I had nearly gotten a lot of people killed for no reason.

Just thinking it made me grit my teeth, and in a way it felt almost as bad as cleaning the fester from my wounded foot. Which was right, because I had to clean out from my mind the fester caused by anger and hatred. I remembered suddenly that horrible day in Galdran's dungeon when the Marquis had come to me himself and offered me a choice between death and surrender. "It might buy you time," he'd said.

At that moment I'd seen surrender as dishonor, and it *had* taken courage to refuse. He'd seen that and had acknowledged it in many different ways, including his words two days before about my being a heroine. Generous words, meant to brace me up. What I saw now was the grim courage it had taken to act his part in Galdran's Court, all the time planning to change things with the least amount of damage to innocent people. And when Branaric and I had come crashing into his plans, he'd included us as much as he could in his net of safety. My subsequent brushes with death were, I saw miserably now, my own fault.

I had to respect what he'd done. He'd come to respect us for our ideals, that much was clear. What he might think of me personally . . .

Suddenly I felt an overwhelming desire to be home. I wanted

badly to clean out our castle, and replant Mama's garden, and walk in the sunny glades, and think, and read, and *learn*. I no longer wanted to face the world in ignorance, wearing castoff clothing and old horse blankets.

But first there was something I had to do.

I slipped out the door; paused, listening. From Branaric's room came the sound of slow, deep breathing. I stepped inside the room Shevraeth had been using, saw a half-folded map on the table, a neat pile of papers, a pen and inkwell, and a folded pair of gloves.

Pulling out the wallet from my clothes, I opened it and extracted Debegri's letter. This I laid on the table beside the papers. Then I knelt down and picked up the pen. Finding a blank sheet of paper, I wrote in slow, careful letters: *You'll probably need this to convince Galdran's old allies.*

Then I retreated to my room, pulled the borrowed tunic over my head, bound up my ratty braid, settled the overlarge hat onto my head, and slipped out the door.

At the end of the little hall was another door, which opened onto a clearing. Under a dilapidated roof waited a string of fine horses, and a few Renselaeus stable hands sat about.

When they saw me, they sprang to their feet.

"My lady?" One bowed.

"I should like a ride," I said, my heart thumping.

But they didn't argue, or refuse, or send someone to warn someone else. Working together, in a trice they had a fine, fresh mare saddled and ready.

And in another trice I was on her back and riding out, on my way home.

"Heee-*oh!*" The call echoed up from the courtyard. "Messenger!"

I straightened up slowly, wincing as my back protested. Skirting my neat piles, I went to the open window and looked down into

205

the sunlit courtyard far below, and saw Oria's younger brother, Calaub, capering excitedly about.

"Just stable the horse and send the messenger in for food, and the message can be left on the table," I called. And, over my shoulder to Oria, "I hope it's my book, but that would be miraculous, for I just sent the letter off—what, three? five? a few days ago."

"It's someone *new!*" Calaub's high voice was a bat squeak of excitement.

I laughed. The children his age had concocted an elaborate spy system to identify anyone coming up the main road to the castle— for no one quite believed, any more than I did, that we were truly safe, despite nearly two months of utter quiet. A quiet that had reigned since the day I rode into Erkan-Astiar on the borrowed mare with my head bandaged and, on my lips, the news that Galdran was truly gone.

Oria looked round the room, which had been Papa's refuge at the end of his life. It had not been touched since his death, and weather and mildew had added to the mess. Not long after my return we had commenced cleaning the castle from the basement up. Papa's room being at the very top of the tallest tower, I had left it for the last.

" 'Tis done," Oria said in satisfaction. She wiped her brow and added, "And not too soon, for the hot weather is nearly on us."

"Which is not the time for fires," I said, looking at the piles of things on the new-swept floor. Most of them were rubbish and would keep us warm at night, for our Fire Sticks had run out of magic. There was some furniture that could be mended, and a very small pile of keepsakes. These last I gathered myself as we went down the steps.

"The twins can bring everything down this afternoon," Oria said. "Mama is eager to get someone up there to scrub. You know she won't declare it's done until every stone is clean."

I set my pile carefully on a small table at the main landing, which was closest to the library. "And then the window work," I said, and bit my lip. We'd have to have shutters to all the windows that had stood open for years, or the place would be full of drafts and dirt by winter. I knew I ought to have glass put in, but I also—desperately—wanted books. So to ease my conscience, I'd decided, as we got the wherewithal, to alternate windows and books, leaving my room for last.

We exited the tower and crossed the courtyard as a quicker route.

No one used the main hall—we all went in and out the side yard, which opened onto the warm kitchens. The spring rains had been tapering off, and though it was full summer in the lowlands, at our heights only of late had we begun feeling a breeze from over the mountains, carrying a warm desert tang from far west. But the nights were still very chill, and often wet.

Oria and I walked into the kitchen to find Julen staring at a handsome young man with curly black hair and fine new livery in Astiar colors.

His chin was up, and he swept a cool glance over us all as he said, "My errand is with my lady, the Countess of Tlanth."

"I am she." I stepped forward.

He gave me one incredulous look, then hastily smoothed his face as he bowed low. In the background, Julen clucked rather audibly. Next to me Oria had her arms crossed, her face stony. The young man looked about with the air of one who knows himself in unfriendly territory, and I reflected that for all his airs my brother had hired him or he wouldn't be here, and he deserved a chance to present himself fair.

"Surely you'll have been warned that we are very informal here," I said, and gave him a big smile.

And for some reason he flushed right up to his fine hairline. Bowing again, he said courteously, "My lady, I was to give this directly to you."

I held out one hand, noticed the dirt smudges, and hastily wiped it on my clothes before putting it out again. When I glanced up at the equerry, I saw in his eyes just a hint of answering amusement at the absurdity of the situation, though his face was strictly schooled when he handed me the letter.

"Welcome among us. What is your name?" I said.

"Jerrol, as it pleases you, my lady." And again the bow.

"Well, it's your name if it pleases me or not," I said, sitting on the edge of the great slate prep table.

Julen clucked again, but softly, and I looked to the side, saw the preparations for tarts lying at the ready, and hastily jumped down again.

"Tell me, Jerrol," I said, "if a great Court lady mislikes the name of a new equerry, will she rename him or her?"

"Like...Frogface or Stenchbelly?" Calaub asked from the open window, and beyond him three or four urchins snickered.

Jerrol glanced about him, his face quite blank, but only for a moment. He then swept me a truly magnificent bow—so flourishing that no one could miss the irony—and he said, "An my lady pleases to address me as Stenchbelly, I shall count myself honored." He pronounced it all with awful elegance.

And everyone laughed! I said, "I think you'll do, Jerrol, for all your clothes are better than any of us have seen for years. But you will have heard something of our affairs, I daresay, and I wonder how my brother managed to hire you, and fit you out this splendidly, in our colors?"

"Wager on it yon letter will explain," Julen said grimly, turning to plunge her hands into her flour.

"Oh!" I had forgotten Jerrol's original purpose for arriving, and looked down at the letter with my name scrawled above the seal in Branaric's careless hand.

Looking down at the stiff, cream-colored rice paper—the good kind that came in the books that we had never been able to afford—I was both excited and apprehensive. Remembering my rather precipitous departure from that wood gatherer's house, I decided that much as I valued my friends, I wanted to read Bran's letter alone.

No one followed me as I walked out. Behind, I heard Oria saying, in a voice very different from what I was used to hearing from her, "Come, Master Jerrol, there's some good ale here, and I'll make you some bread and cheese..."

As I walked up to my room, I reflected on the fact that I *did* want to read it alone, and not have whatever it said read from my face. Then there was the fact that they all let me go off alone without a word said, though I knew they wanted to know what was in it.

It's that invisible barrier again, I thought, feeling peculiar. *We can work all day at the same tasks, bathe together at the village bathhouse, and sit down together at meals, but then something comes up and suddenly I'm the Astiar and they are the vassals... just as at the village dances all the best posies and the finest plates are brought to me, but the young men all talk and laugh with the other girls.*

Was this, then, to be my life? To always feel suspended midway between the aristocrat and the vassal traditions, and to belong truly to neither?

I sat down in my quiet room and worked my finger under the seal.

Dear Mel:

I trust this finds you recovered. Why did you have to run off like that? But I figured you were safe arrived at home, and well, or Khesot would've sent to me here—since you wouldn't write.

And how was I to pay for sending a letter to Remalna-city? I thought indignantly, then sighed. Of course, I *had* managed to find enough coin to write to Ara's family, and to obtain through the father the name of a good bookseller. But the first was an obligation, I told myself. And as for the latter, it was merely the start of the education that Branaric had blabbed to the world that I lacked.

I'm here at Athanarel, finding it to my taste. It helps that Galdran's personal fortune has been turned over to us, as repayment for what happened to our family—you'll find the Letter of Intent in with this letter, to be kept somewhere safe. Henceforth, you send your creditors for drafts on Arclor House . . .

I looked up at the ceiling as the words slowly sank in. "Personal fortune"? How much was that? Whatever it was, it had to be a vast improvement over our present circumstances. I grinned, thinking how I had agonized over which book to choose from the bookseller's list. Now I could order them all. I could even hire my own scribe . . .

Shaking my head, I banished the dreams of avarice, and returned to the letter—not that much remained.

. . . so, outfit yourself in whatever you want, appoint someone responsible as steward, and join me here at Athanarel as soon as you can. Everyone here wants to meet you.

"Now, that's a frightening thought," I said grimly.

And I think it's time for you to make your peace with Vidanric.

He ended with a scrawled signature.

I lowered the letter slowly to the desk, not wanting to consider why I found that last suggestion even more frightening than the first.

Behind Bran's letter, bearing three official-looking seals, was the Letter of Intent. In very beautiful handwriting, it named in precise terms a sum even higher than I'd dared to let myself think of, the remainder after the taxes for the army had been subtracted. Wondering who was getting *that* sum, which was even greater, I scanned the rest, which outlined in flowery language pretty much what Branaric had said. It seemed we now had a business house handling our money; previously I'd gathered the scanty sums and redispersed them myself, in coin.

I put that letter down, too. Suddenly the possibilities now available started multiplying in my mind. Not visiting Athanarel. I didn't even consider that; I'd tried to win a crown, and lost. But supposedly all the wrongs I had fought for were being addressed, and so—I vowed—I was done with royal affairs.

No, I told myself, my work now was Tlanth, and with this money, all my plans could be put into action. Rebuilding, new roads, booksellers . . . I looked around at the castle, no longer seeing the weather damage and neglect, but how it would look repaired and redecorated.

"Oria!" I yelled, running downstairs. "Oria! Julen! Calaub! We're *rich*!"

EPILOGUE

I MEANT THAT LITERALLY, TOO, FOR RIGHT FROM the start I regarded that not as our fortune, but as Tlanth's.

Within the space of a month I had an army of artisans up on the mountain working—traveling back and forth over the new-paved roads. Not just the castle but also the villages, all of them, were getting roads and roofs and windows and whatever else was needed. The prosperity was not just a short-lived one, for it stimulated business, and business in turn stimulated vigorous trade with the lowlands.

I officially appointed Oria the steward of the castle, a job she embraced so enthusiastically that for a while we were *all* camping out under the stars as she went through the castle again, this time reordering everything. The results were better than I could have imagined.

Julen received from me all the years' wages she should have gotten. She didn't say much, but I noted later that young Calaub (who was now a stable boy, something he'd desperately wanted) had his own horse, and the blacksmith's shop sported new equipment. As for Julen, she didn't dress differently, or talk more, but she was over at the castle helping her daughter with a kind of smiling determination that I'd never seen before. To Azmus and Khesot, now honorably retired from war, I gave money to buy their own houses. Khesot planted fruit trees, and Azmus went back to goldsmithing.

The one thing I reserved for myself was the purchase of books—though even that was not just for myself. The steady arrival of books filled the new shelves in the castle library, but I made it clear that they were there for the asking. Anyone who wished an education could join me in banishing ignorance.

My quest for an education very soon turned into a thirst for knowledge for its own sake. I discovered in histories the voices of other men and women who shared hard-won wisdom through the recounting of their life experiences, or through the careful retelling of the lives of others.

I still wandered about in scruffy clothes scrounged from old chests and closets, for my days were too filled to take the time to have new ones made. I was overseeing all aspects of the rebuilding, usually with a book tucked under my arm in case I found myself with a bit of free time. Before the war, an unexpected free afternoon had meant I could run to the hills, but now unoccupied moments usually found me curled up reading on my new cushions in the library, or writing down notes on what I had read.

As the days shortened and the winds from the east turned cold, Branaric still lingered in the capital. My thoughts thus often turned southward to Athanarel and the Court, and I wondered what he was doing there, and how he was getting along. And though I had reread his letter so often I'd memorized it, I still had not answered. What stopped me were his words about unfinished business.

Someday, I knew, I would have to resolve that business, but not—so I reasoned—as the ignorant country-bumpkin countess. If I ever went to Court I would face the people there on equal terms.

In the meantime it was good to walk about and see Tlanth prospering. Soon winter would come, and I liked to envision everyone, from high to low degree, snug and warm in well-built houses, looking out on the snowy mountaintops and hearing the windharps of the Hill Folk singing of peace.